Charlie stared at him. 'He wants you to go to Ecuador? But you can't go shooting off at such short notice! What about your book?'

'It's a damned shame,' he agreed. 'But I've already told him I'll go. I'm not sure when I'll be back in England again—I'm off on a lecture tour of America in a couple of months—so it looks as if the book will have to be abandoned indefinitely.'

'Your friend's got a pretty poor sense of timing,' Charlie commented. 'I suppose the only solution would be to take me with you,' she added jokingly. 'Then we could work on the book whenever you've got some free time.' Inwardly, though, she didn't feel in the least amused. It looked as if her feature story had come to an abrupt end before it had even got off the ground. Then she looked up and found Jay Challoner's gaze was fixed on her with new thoughtfulness.

'Is your passport up to date?' he asked.

Charlie smiled. The man certainly had a sense of humour! Then she realised he wasn't smiling back at her. And that was when her own eyes began to open wide in stunned disbelief...

ILLUSION
OF PARADISE

BY

JOANNA MANSELL

MILLS & BOON LIMITED
ETON HOUSE   18-24 PARADISE ROAD
RICHMOND   SURREY   TW9 1SR

*First published in Great Britain 1988
by Mills & Boon Limited*

© Joanna Mansell 1988

*Australian copyright 1988
Philippine copyright 1988
This edition 1988*

ISBN 0 263 75955 5

*Set in Times Roman 10 on 11¼ pt.
01-0488-58583 C*

*Printed and bound in Great Britain by
Collins, Glasgow*

CHAPTER ONE

CHARLIE glanced at her watch, then stared anxiously up the road. Damn! Why weren't there ever any taxis around when you needed one?

Then she spotted one turning the corner. Letting out a huge sigh of relief, she shot out into the middle of the road, forcing the taxi to screech to a halt a couple of yards in front of her.

The driver stuck his head out of the window and glared at her. 'You certainly like living dangerously, lady!'

Charlie shoved a piece of paper under his nose. 'I've got to be at this address by eleven o'clock. Can you get me there on time?'

'I'm off duty. You'll have to find another taxi.'

She flashed him her most dazzling smile, the one that made her face look all huge eyes and delectable mouth. 'But I'm going for an interview for a job. It really is *very* important.'

The taxi driver stared at her for a couple more seconds, then visibly melted. A moment later, he flicked on the 'For Hire' sign. 'All right, in you get.'

Charlie promptly scrambled into the back. 'Will we be there by eleven? I mustn't be late.'

'Don't panic, we'll make it with time to spare,' he told her, his tone much more good-natured now. 'What kind of job are you going for?'

'It's secretarial work. The job's only temporary, but I really need to get it.'

'Money's short?' sympathised the taxi driver.

'Let's just say that getting this job could make a whole lot of difference to my career,' Charlie answered, slightly evasively.

They hit some heavy traffic at that point and, as the driver concentrated on weaving his way through the lines of buses and cars, Charlie stared out of the window and tried to relax. She hadn't been joking when she had told the driver that getting this temporary secretarial job could be vitally important to her career. Dan Marshall, her editor, had made it perfectly clear yesterday that he was counting on her to pull off this assignment.

When he had first told her about it, Charlie had simply stared at him blankly.

'But how on earth can I do a big feature story on Jay Challoner?' she asked. 'He doesn't give interviews, everyone knows that.'

Dan Marshall shot her an exasperated glance. 'I'm not suggesting that you walk up to his front door and ask him straight out for an interview! You're going to have to find some other way of digging up the information you'll need for the story.' Then he leant forward a few inches. 'Look, Charlie, the magazine's doing well, the circulation figures are holding up better than anyone originally forecast. But we need to push them up even higher if we're going to make it into the big league. And an exclusive feature on Jay Challoner could just pull in those extra readers.'

Charlie absently flicked back a silky strand of her blonde hair. 'All I'll probably be able to dig up are those few facts that everyone already knows,' she warned. 'That's not going to make much of a feature.'

Dan tapped the side of his nose, then grinned. 'Don't worry, I've already found a way round that problem. I've got a lot of useful contacts, and one of them's just come up with the interesting fact that Jay Challoner's looking for a temporary secretary. He's holding interviews in his hotel suite tomorrow morning. All you've got to do is get over there and make sure that you're the girl he takes on. Get that job, and you'll be able to snoop around without him suspecting a thing. Once you're working for him, there should be all sorts of opportunities to ferret out enough material for a sensational feature.'

Charlie frowned. 'That's sneaky, Dan.'

'Of course it is,' he agreed, without the faintest hint of an apology in his voice. When it came to getting an exclusive story, Dan was like most editors. He didn't let a little thing like scruples stand in his way.

'Anyway, there's a good chance I might not even get the job,' she argued.

'You'll get it,' he said confidently. 'You've got excellent shorthand and typing speeds. And as well as that, you're a blonde. I've heard that Challoner likes blondes.'

Charlie stared at him in exasperation. 'You're impossible!'

'That's what my wife keeps telling me,' he replied with a grin. Then he became briskly efficient again. 'This story is important,' he emphasised. 'I *want* it. The first in-depth feature on Jay Challoner—it should give an enormous boost to our circulation.' He scribbled something down on a piece of paper, then handed it to her. 'This is the address of Challoner's hotel. Make sure you're there at eleven, and that you get the job.' He paused briefly, then added, 'I suppose you have read the man's books?'

'Er—no, I haven't,' Charlie admitted, slightly guiltily.

Dan sighed, reached into the drawer of his desk, took out two books and pushed them over to her. Charlie saw Challoner's name of the covers, and silently groaned when she saw how thick they were.

'You'd better take the rest of the day off,' Dan advised. 'Read the books so you've got some idea of the

type of man you'll be dealing with. One more thing—
he's a professor of anthropology, so it might make a
good impression on him if you address him as Professor.
Sometimes a little formal courtesy can go a long way.'

'You wouldn't like me to curtsy to him as well, would
you?' enquired Charlie with a touch of sarcasm.

Dan shot her a warning glance and she promptly shut
up, grabbed hold of the books, and hurriedly left the
office.

Once back in her flat, she made herself a light lunch,
then flopped down on the sofa and picked up one of
Jay Challoner's books. She had heard of them, of
course—who hadn't, after all the weeks they had spent
at the top of the best-selling charts? She preferred fiction
to non-fiction, though, so she had never actually got
around to reading them. She knew roughly what they
were about, however. Jay Challoner had been a lecturer
at one of the top universities, but he had apparently
grown tired of the restrictions of the academic life. He
had thrown in his job, then launched out on a couple
of distinctly offbeat anthropological experiments of his
own devising.

For his initial venture, chronicled in detail in his first
book, he and his current girlfriend had gone off to live
with a group of Eskimos, enduring the rigours of an
Arctic winter, a monotonous diet, and the constant,
bone-freezing cold. The book had been not just a vivid
account of the life-style that was rapidly disappearing,
but of Jay's and his girlfriend's struggle to adapt to a
way of life that was relentlessly tough and totally alien.
At the end of the winter, his girlfriend had left him, and
Jay himself had nearly died of exposure after getting
lost out on the ice, only being found in the nick of time
by a couple of Eskimos.

The second book was quite different, although no less
riveting. This time, Jay had advertised for a girl to ac-

company him to Central Africa, where he was embarking on a detailed study of one of the primitive tribes, living among them for several months, quite out of touch with civilisation. At the same time, he planned to run a very different kind of experiment, involving the girl who went with him. The main purpose was to discover how a girl used to all modern conveniences and luxuries would cope when suddenly thrown into a totally primitive environment.

The theme of the book was simple. How adaptable was the 'modern woman'? Underneath the glossy, sophisticated surface, did she still have all the instincts that she needed to survive in difficult, even dangerous, circumstances? Could she adapt quickly, learn to live without electricity and running water, become self-sufficient, overcome hardship and deprivation?

The answer seemed to be a resounding 'yes'. The girl Jay had finally chosen from the hundreds who had applied had proved resourceful, strong-minded and resilient.

But the most fascinating section of the book hadn't been the account of the physical hardships they had endured, including the fraught period when supplies of food had run perilously low and they, along with the rest of the tribe, had lived for several weeks on the edge of starvation. Instead, it was the relentlessly detailed account of the relationship that had developed between the two of them, the joys, the highs and lows it had gone through before finally falling irrevocably apart, leaving them no longer lovers, and barely even friends.

Once they had returned to civilisation and the book had been published, the girl had become an overnight celebrity. With none of Jay Challoner's reservations about seeking publicity, she had cashed in on her moment of fame. Charlie remembered seeing her on several chat shows, and knew that she had now taken herself off to Hollywood, chasing up offers of film parts.

When Charlie finally put down the second book, she sat and stared uneasily ahead of her for several long minutes. She had thought the books were just going to be straightforward adventure stories that had been deliberately spiced up to make them sell. The overriding impression she had been left with, though, was that this man, Jay Challoner, liked to take people apart, to find out what made them tick. She wasn't at all sure that she liked that. Deep inside her, she could feel a definite niggle of unease. Eventually, she reached for the phone. Dan often worked late at the office. With luck, she could catch him before he went home.

When she heard his voice on the other end, she bit her lower lip a little edgily. 'Dan, I'm not sure I can cope with this assignment. Do you know what this Jay Challoner does? He shoves people into unusual situations, sits back and watches them, then he—he *dissects* them.'

'He *is* an anthropologist,' Dan reminded her. 'The way I see it, he's just interested in the way people behave when they're put into an environment that's totally different from the one they're used to. To be honest, I think it's pretty fascinating stuff. So do millions of others, judging by the phenomenal sales of his books. Anyway, what's this got to do with your assignment? All I'm asking you to do is to make sure you get that job as his temporary secretary. Once you're working alongside him, you shouldn't have any problems getting enough material for your feature.'

'I just don't like it. The man who wrote these books isn't an idiot; he's quite capable of seeing right through my cover story,' Charlie retorted, that odd quiver of nerves still making her touchy.

'Rubbish,' Dan responded firmly. 'Just bat those beautiful blue eyes of yours at him—he'll be so dazzled, he won't suspect a thing. Remember, Charlie,' he warned, 'I'm counting on you to pull this off. I shan't be particularly pleased if you come back and tell me you've blown it.'

And so here she was, sitting in the taxi, on her way to an interview with Jay Challoner. That uncomfortable niggle of unease was still squirming around inside her stomach and, despite her bright smile, she definitely wasn't happy about this assignment.

The taxi screeched to a halt outside the hotel at five minutes to eleven. Charlie thanked the driver, hurriedly paid him, then dashed into the hotel. On the way up in the lift, she quickly checked her hair and make-up; then she scurried along the corridor to Jay Challoner's suite. She knocked on the door, but when there was no reply she turned the handle and tentatively opened it.

A second later, her mouth fell open. The room inside was crammed absolutely full of girls, nearly all of them gorgeous, and most of them blondes. Honey-blondes, strawberry-blondes, platinum, sun-streaked and high-lighted blondes. Word had definitely got around which colour Jay Challoner preferred!

'Shove up, everyone, another one's just arrived!' yelled out the girl nearest the door. A collective groan went up, but the girls eventually shuffled a little closer together, leaving just enough room for Charlie to squeeze inside.

'Are you all here for the interviews for the secretarial job?' Charlie asked rather incredulously.

The girl grinned. 'Most of us are hoping Jay Challoner's looking for more than just a secretary,' she admitted.

Charlie shot her a puzzled look. 'What do you mean?'

'Come on, there's no need to act the innocent. We're all here for the same reason. There's a rumour going round that Jay Challoner's planning another book, and just about every girl in this room would give her right arm for the chance to be featured in it. After all, look what happened to the girl in his last book,' she sighed enviously. 'TV shows, film contracts—instant stardom!'

Oh, Dan, what on earth have you got me into? Charlie asked herself with a small groan. And what was it about this Jay Challoner? It looked as if someone only had to mention his name, and handfuls of stunning blondes started to pop out of the woodwork.

Just then, the door opened behind her. Charlie couldn't believe that one more person could push their way into this overcrowded room. They were already crammed in like sardines; if any more girls tried to squeeze in, the walls would start to bulge! All the same, she took a deep breath. Then she good-naturedly pushed forward a little, trying to make room for the new arrival. A few seconds later, she realised that the rest of the girls had suddenly gone very quiet, and that every pair of eyes in the room seemed to have swivelled round, fixing on some point just behind her.

Puzzled, she twisted round to see what had caused this odd reaction. Then she gulped a trifle nervously as she saw the tall, broad male figure that was now completely filling the doorway.

There had been a small black and white photo of Jay Challoner on the back covers of his books, but it hadn't borne very much resemblance to the man who now stood in front of her. For one thing, it hadn't revealed that his eyes were different colours, one green and one blue. Quite extraordinary!

The green eye winked at her.

'I can wink the blue one as well,' he murmured in a low voice that only she could hear. And he did.

Charlie blushed furiously. She hadn't realised she had been staring at his odd-coloured eyes with such curiosity.

Jay Challoner moved back slightly, then surveyed the packed roomful of girls.

'All right,' he said, raising his voice so that everyone could hear him, 'it's far too crowded in here. I can't even get in the door. Let's have you all out in the corridor, where there's more room.'

He paced up and down, slightly restlessly, as the girls milled out into the corridor, lining themselves up along both walls. Charlie couldn't help noticing that his gaze flickered appreciatively over a couple of tall blondes who were stunningly attractive. This was getting to be distinctly humiliating, she told herself with growing indignation as she took her place at the very end of the line-up. Jay Challoner looked as if he was browsing through a row of books, to see if he could find something interesting that caught his eye—except that he was actually browsing through girls!

All the same, she was unexpectedly disturbed by her first encounter with Jay Challoner. He was a great bear of a man, tall and broad, yet definitely not lumbering— far from it. He didn't walk, he prowled, that large, powerful body moving with a smooth suppleness that she found—well, slightly alarming, she admitted to herself rather uneasily. She had the feeling that he could move very fast if he wanted to, despite his size; that it would be almost impossible to escape from him if he decided that he didn't want to let you go. At the same time, he seemed to radiate great waves of energy. Charlie was left with the unexpectedly vivid impression of a man who had spent much of his adult life searching for outlets for that pent-up energy, and the colourful imagination which accompanied it.

He strode up the corridor one last time; then he stood at the far end and surveyed the two lines of girls.

'Thank you all for turning up this morning. Let's hope it hasn't been a waste of both your time and mine. Despite all the rumours going around at the moment, all I'm looking for right now is a temporary secretary.' At that, a low murmur of disappointment spread along the corridor, and Jay Challoner drily lifted one eyebrow. 'So, now we've got that straight, let's get down to basics. I'm looking for someone who can take dictation at around a hundred words a minute, and type it back fast and accurately. If any of you are qualified along those lines, perhaps you'd be good enough to step forward.'

Out of all the girls in the corridor, only three detached themselves from the line-up. Two rather plain brunettes, and Charlie.

'The three of you had better come inside,' Jay Challoner instructed briskly. 'The rest of you—thanks for coming, but I won't be needing you.'

Charlie and the other two girls followed him into his suite. Then she had to sit and wait while he interviewed the other two girls first in an adjoining room. Finally, it was her turn. As she walked into the other room, she found Jay Challoner sitting behind a small desk. At least, it wasn't really a small desk, it was just that his large body seemed to dwarf it. She slid into the chair on the other side, then stared up into those disconcerting bi-coloured eyes.

'Perhaps you'd like to begin by introducing yourself,' he suggested.

'I'm Charlotte Franklin. Everyone calls me Charlie, though,' she said rather nervously.

'Charlie?' he repeated, one green eye and one blue eye fixing on her thoughtfully. 'I don't think that suits you at all. You don't look in the least like a boy to me. I'll stick to Charlotte, if you don't mind.'

As a matter of fact, she did mind. She minded very much. Only one other person had ever insisted on calling

her Charlotte, and just hearing the full version of her
name caused her nerves to give a sharp, painful twist.
She could hardly begin this interview with a full-scale
argument over what she was to be called, though, so she
swallowed hard and tried not to let any of her inner
turmoil show on her face.

'Are you with one of the main secretarial agencies?'
he asked.

'No, I work free-lance,' Charlie lied smoothly. 'I heard
about this job through a friend, and I turned up on the
off-chance that I'd be lucky. Would you like to see my
certificates?' She took them out of her bag and pushed
them towards him.

Jay Challoner only glanced at them briefly. 'On paper,
you're certainly well qualified, but I always think a
practical test is the best measure of someone's ability.
Would you mind taking a few minutes' dictation, then
reading it back to me?'

'Of course not,' she agreed. She fished a notebook
and pencil out of her bag, and hoped she looked a lot
more cool and efficient than she felt on the inside.

He read a short passage from a book on the desk,
dictating quickly but clearly. She got it down without
any problems, then read it back to him in an equally
clear voice.

'That seems fine,' he nodded, when she had finally
finished. 'Now, how about a few personal details?'

Charlie's nerves gave another sharp twitch. 'Personal
details?' she echoed, slightly uneasily.

'For a start, are you free for the next three or four
weeks?'

'Oh—yes, I've no other commitments at the moment.'

'It's possible I might want you for rather longer than
that,' he warned. 'If you take this job, would that cause
any problems?'

'None at all,' she assured him. It didn't really matter what she agreed to, she told herself. Once she had got the material for her feature, she could make some excuse and just walk out. He wouldn't find it difficult to replace her.

'One other thing,' he went on. 'I don't intend to stay in London—I'm going to move down to my house on the coast for the next few weeks. There's no way you'd be able to commute every day, so it would mean you'd have to live in while you're working for me. Would you have any objections to that? One part of the house has been converted to a small, self-contained flat, so we wouldn't be under each other's feet out of working hours.'

Charlie tried hard to keep the bright glitter of anticipation out of her eyes. Would she object to seeing Jay Challoner in his home environment? Definitely not! It would give her a fantastic background for her feature.

'That would be fine by me,' she answered immediately.

He settled back in his chair and looked at her thoughtfully. 'Why do you want this job?' he asked unexpectedly.

Charlie was thrown a little off balance by his blunt question.

'I thought it would—well—that it would be—interesting,' she waffled at last, rather lamely.

'Interesting?' he prompted gently.

'Your books are so—fascinating,' she burbled on. 'I thought it would be really great to work for you, even if the job is only temporary.'

Oh, this was ridiculous! she told herself with a touch of exasperation. She was beginning to sound like a half-wit. If she carried on like this much longer, he was going to lose patience and give the job to someone else. Why on earth had she suddenly started to gabble like some star-struck adolescent? It must be something to do with the man himself, he looked so—so big, so *daunting*, sitting there on the other side of the desk and staring directly at her with those peculiar eyes.

A faint frown was beginning to draw his dark brows together. 'Do I make you nervous?' he demanded a moment later, still studying her face with disconcerting keenness.

'Make me nervous?' she echoed, with a rather poor attempt at a casual laugh. 'No, of course not.'

'I *am* making you nervous,' he said, his frown deepening. 'Why?'

Since Charlie could hardly admit that she was finding it unexpectedly hard to keep up this string of half-truths and white lies, she flashed him the brilliant smile which had got her out of awkward situations so many times in the past.

'You're so famous,' she explained. 'I suppose I'm a bit—well, overwhelmed.'

And if he swallowed that, he would swallow anything, she told herself drily. Yet incredibly, he didn't query her answer. Instead, he gazed at her speculatively for a few more moments. Then he finally gave a brief shrug, as if he had suddenly lost interest in that particular line of questioning.

'Perhaps I'd better explain the kind of work you'd be doing, then you can tell me if you're interested. I'm taking a few weeks' break, and I thought it would be relaxing to try a different kind of writing, something that's pure fiction. I've had an idea floating around in the back of my mind for some time now, so I'm going to see how it works out once it's set down on paper.'

Charlie blinked in disbelief. That was this man's idea of relaxation? To sit down and write a novel? Then the full implication of what he was telling her abruptly sank in. She would have all the inside information on Jay Challoner's next book—what a scoop!

'Are you actually offering me the job?' she breathed, hardly able to believe her luck.

Jay Challoner nodded. 'If you want it. You might find it extremely boring, though,' he warned. 'It's going to be, basically, a lot of dictation and straight copy typing.'

'I won't be bored,' she assured him eagerly. Then she couldn't stop herself asking, 'Why did you offer it to me, instead of one of the other two girls?'

One dark eyebrow lifted gently. 'You want the truth?' When she nodded, he shot her an amused glance and went on. 'If I have to have a temporary secretary, I thought I might as well have one who's pleasant to look at. I'm well aware that's a completely chauvinistic attitude,' he went on, his mouth twisting into a faintly mocking grin, 'but I've no intention of apologising for it. And don't worry—I'll only look, I won't touch. That's a promise.' He stared straight at her with a distinctly challenging light in his eyes. 'Do you still want the job?'

'Yes,' Charlie said at once, firmly ignoring the faint warning signals that were racing along her nerve-ends.

'I'll be driving down to the coast on Monday,' he told her. 'If you like, I'll pick you up and you can drive down with me.'

'Thank you, but I'd prefer to come in my own car,' she replied, determined to establish her independence right from the very start.

He shrugged. 'As you please.' He gave her the address, and precise instructions on how to get there. Then he got to his feet, clearly signalling that the interview was over. 'I'll look forward to seeing you next Monday.'

'I'll be there,' Charlie promised. But, as she left his hotel suite, she couldn't get rid of the feeling that this assignment wasn't going to work out quite the way she had expected.

* * *

When she reported the success of her interview to Dan Marshall, his face relaxed into a huge smile of satisfaction.

'I knew you could pull this off, Charlie. And you say Challoner's starting work on another book? This could work out even better than I thought. We might even end up getting serial rights.'

Charlie frowned. 'Why on earth would he give us serial rights? I've got this job as his secretary just so I can dig around in his private life for information for my feature. When he finds out how I tricked him, he's going to be absolutely furious. The very last thing he's going to want to do is give us the rights to his next book.'

'That could well depend on the kind of article you finally produce,' Dan said, still beaming cheerfully. 'Come up with something really good, and Challoner might like it so much that he'll look favourably on any bid we put in for his book.'

Charlie thought Dan was definitely being over-optimistic. And, as she packed her bags the following weekend, she firmly squashed any lingering scruples she had about the way she was going about getting this story. Three years ago, she would never have dreamt of doing anything like this, of lying her way into someone's house, someone's life, just so she could get the material for a first-rate feature. She was a lot tougher, a lot harder now, though. And the fact that none of that inner hardness showed on the outside was a real asset, as far as she was concerned. Hardly anyone saw beyond her big, innocent blue eyes, the deceptively pretty face with its dazzling smile, the silky fall of pale blonde hair that gave her a deceptive air of fragility.

She used those assets quite ruthlessly in order to get the stories she was after. Why not? It was a tough world; she had always known that, and what had happened to her three years ago had only confirmed that belief, etching it on her mind so clearly that nothing could erase it. Sometimes, she was faintly appalled by the cynical attitude that had crept over her these last couple of years. Then her face would set into an uncharacteristically hard expression, and she would deliberately put any qualms behind her. It wasn't *her* fault she had changed. And, since it was quite impossible for her to go back to the way she had been before, she just had to get on with her life as best she could.

On Monday morning, the sun was shining brightly as she drove down to the coast. Jay Challoner's directions were easy to follow. In a couple of hours, she was turning off down a narrow lane and sending the car zooming towards the solitary house she could see in the distance, perched perilously close to the edge of a sheer cliff. On either side, high headlands jutted out into the sea, which sparkled as the sunlight hit it, and the view in all directions was fairly spectacular.

Charlie drew the car to a halt on the drive in front of the house; then she peered down. The nearest houses were at least a couple of miles away, and she grimaced. Friendly chats with the neighbours were definitely out; it looked as if she would be living like a hermit for the next couple of weeks.

Jay Challoner was waiting for her, and he immediately took her up to the first floor, to show her the rooms she would be using. She was relieved to find he had told her the truth. She would be living in a completely self-contained unit, with its own bathroom and small kitchen.

'It was originally designed as a granny-flat,' he told her, 'and I didn't alter it when I bought the house. I thought it would be useful to have somewhere where friends could have a little privacy when they came to stay.'

'Do you have many visitors?' she asked curiously.

He gave an unexpected grin. 'Quite a few. I enjoy peace and quiet, but I certainly don't live like a recluse. That reminds me—if you want to invite someone down to stay at weekends, when you're not working, I certainly won't have any objections. My own rooms are on the other side of the house, so you won't disturb me.'

Charlie stiffened slightly. 'Thank you, but I won't be asking anyone to stay,' she told him rather coldly.

Jay looked faintly surprised. 'No boyfriend?'

'No,' Charlie responded with some terseness.

His dark brows drew together thoughtfully. 'Have I hit some tender spot? You're not in the middle of some traumatic divorce or tangled legal separation, are you?'

'Definitely not,' came her instant response. 'As a matter of fact, I'm a widow.'

Her mouth snapped shut again. Why the hell had she told him that? She never discussed her private life with anyone. And anyway, what a ridiculous way it was to describe herself! Girls her age weren't widows; widows were sad-eyed, older women who had lost husbands of many years' standing, while her own marriage had lasted barely six months.

Jay Challoner was studying her now in a way that made her feel distinctly uncomfortable. 'You must have had a rough time,' he said at last. 'An experience like that always leaves scars of some kind.'

At that, she very nearly laughed out loud. Scars? Oh, yes, it had left scars! Then she somehow got control of herself again, and she forced her face to remain deliberately blank.

'I'm over it now,' she told him abruptly. 'And I really don't want to talk about it. If you'll give me half an hour to get unpacked, I'll be ready to start work.'

He looked at her curiously but, to her relief, he didn't say anything more. Instead, he left her to unpack. Forcefully dragging her frayed nerves back into order,

Charlie concentrated on putting her things away into the ample cupboard space, refusing to let herself think about their conversation.

It didn't take her long to get settled in, and she began work directly after lunch. The room Jay had set aside for her to work in faced the sea and, since it had huge picture windows, it was a severe temptation to just sit and soak up the impressive view.

For the first couple of days, all she did was type up and try to sort into some kind of order the pages of hand-scribbled notes that were piled on her desk. There was background research, odd pages of dialogue, rough character sketches, scrawled chapter outlines, and a lot of technical data which she didn't even understand. It wasn't long before she realised that Jay Challoner's first novel was going to be a thriller of some sort.

Jay himself sometimes worked in the room with her, thumbing his way through piles of books as he searched for odd snippets of information he needed. More often, though, he abandoned his desk and went striding off along the clifftop on solitary rambles.

'I think more clearly when I'm walking,' he admitted one morning.

'Just as long as you don't expect me to run along beside you, taking dictation on the move,' she retorted with raised eyebrows.

'It probably wouldn't be a very practical way of working,' he agreed with a grin. Then he looked at her a little more closely. 'Are you going to frown like that all day?' he enquired.

'It's your handwriting!' Charlie told him in exasperation. 'It's enough to make anyone frown. It looks like a drunken spider's fallen into an inkpot, then staggered its way across the page. Look at that,' she said, holding up the page she had been poring over. 'It would take a code-breaking expert to decipher it!'

Jay was about to take the sheet of paper from her when the phone rang in the hall outside. 'Back in a moment,' he promised, and she gave an impatient sigh, then peered irritably at the page of scrawled writing once more.

It was quite some time before he finally returned and, when he did, his brows were drawn together in a slight frown.

'Problems?' she asked, glancing up at him.

'In a way. That was Jim Fielding, a friend of mine, and a fellow anthropologist. He was phoning from Quito. That's in Ecuador—South America,' he added helpfully.

'I know where Ecuador is,' Charlie replied, a little indignantly. 'What's your friend doing in Quito?'

'Very little,' Jay commented drily. 'He's lying in a hospital bed, virtually immobile. He had a fall a few days ago, and injured his back and leg. He's going to be in the hospital for at least three or four weeks, perhaps even longer.'

'That's a shame, but what's it got to do with you?'

'Jim was doing a year-long survey on one of the tribes of Indians in a remote part of the rain forest,' Jay explained. 'He was making a complete record of their lifestyle over the entire year. If he loses a month while he's in hospital, then obviously the survey's going to be incomplete.'

'Is it really important to know all about the lives of some obscure tribe of Indians?' asked Charlie, without much interest.

Jay's eyes altered perceptibly. 'When so-called civilisation's doing its best to wipe out their traditional way of life completely, I would say it's very important. We're cutting down the rain forests of the world at a disastrous and horrifying rate. In a couple more generations, these Indians' environment could have been totally destroyed. A lot of people are trying very hard to stop it happening but, if they fail, at least we'll have a record of the people who once lived there. They won't have been forgotten completely, as if they never even existed.'

A little shaken by his vehemence—and rather ashamed by her own lack of understanding—Charlie slowly nodded. 'Yes, I can appreciate that. No wonder your friend's upset at being stuck in a hospital bed.'

'He doesn't give up easily, though,' Jay said. 'That's why he's rung me and asked if I'll go out and take his place, carry on the survey until he's on his feet again.'

Charlie stared at him. 'He wants you to go to Ecuador? But you can't go shooting off at such short notice! What about your book?'

'It's a damned shame,' he agreed. 'But I've already told him I'll go. I'm not sure when I'll be back in England again—I'm off on a lecture tour of America in a couple of months—so it looks as if the book will have to be abandoned indefinitely.'

'Your friend's got a pretty poor sense of timing,' Charlie commented. 'You've done all the background work and research, and now you've got to abandon it just when you're ready to start actually writing it. I suppose the only solution would be to take me with you,' she added jokingly. 'Then we could work on the book whenever you've got some free time.' Inwardly, though, she didn't feel in the least amused. It looked as if her feature story had come to an abrupt end before it had even got off the ground. It was completely frustrating, to say the least.

She looked up, and found Jay Challoner's gaze was fixed on her with new thoughtfulness.

'Is your passport up to date?' he asked.

Charlie smiled. The man certainly had a sense of humour! Then she realised that he wasn't smiling back at her. And that was when her own eyes began to open very wide in stunned disbelief.

Much later that day, she skulked in the kitchen until she heard Jay going out for another of his long walks. Then she bolted into the hall, grabbed the phone, and dialled the number of Dan's office.

When he picked up the receiver, she didn't even give him the chance to say hello. She just jumped in straight away.

'Dan, Jay Challoner's shooting off to South America, and he wants to take me with him, all expenses paid. It's the craziest idea, how on earth can he sit in the middle of the jungle and write a book? I can't possibly go, of course——'

'Charlie, you're gabbling!' Dan interrupted her. 'Let's get this straight. Challoner's going to South America?'

'A friend of his was doing a study of this tribe of Indians, but now he's in hospital and he wants Jay to stand in for him. Jay's got this insane idea about taking me along, so he can work on his book at the same time——'

'What on earth made him think of that?'

'Well, I suppose I put the idea into his head,' Charlie admitted reluctantly. 'But I only said it as a joke; I didn't think for a moment he'd take the whole thing seriously!'

'It's a brilliant idea,' Dan enthused happily. 'You'll be able to see the man at work, and it'll add a whole new depth to your feature. Call into the photographic department before you leave, and we'll fix you up with a couple of cameras. Then, with luck, we'll get some pictures to go along with the feature.'

'But I could be away from the office for weeks,' she objected a little desperately.

'Do you think the magazine's going to close down without you?' he asked reasonably.

'But South America——'

'I don't care if the guy's going to the North Pole,' Dan came back instantly. 'You stick to Challoner like glue, Charlie, until you get that story.'

He put the phone down before she had a chance to splutter out any more objections, and she stared at the receiver disbelievingly for a couple of minutes, before finally hanging up.

Ecuador—with Jay Challoner—the whole idea was totally insane! No one in their right mind would go to these lengths just to get a story. As soon as Jay got back, she would tell him she couldn't possibly go with him.

Of course, it would probably mean that Dan would sack her. And it wouldn't be easy to find another job.

Charlie sighed. She was a city girl; the thought of sitting in the middle of a rain forest surrounded by a lot of trees totally depressed her. Anyway, she had a bad feeling about this assignment; it had been there right from the beginning. She was quite sure it was going to lurch steadily on towards complete disaster. If she had any sense, she would pull out of it right now.

And end up on the dole? Another out-of-work journalist?

She sighed again, and wondered what she ought to pack for an indefinite stay in the jungle.

CHAPTER TWO

CHARLIE stared out of the window of the small plane
and gave herself the twelfth pinch in the last hour, still
trying to convince herself she wasn't dreaming. The mile
upon mile of thick green forest beneath them didn't go
away, though. In the end, she gave a small shake of her
head and glumly accepted that she was actually here,
somewhere in the depths of Ecuador.

She had never seen so many trees in one place. They
seemed to stretch from horizon to horizon, the sea of
greenness only broken by the pale, mud-coloured rivers
that wound their way through in a complicated pattern
of huge twists and loops.

'Impressive, isn't it?' commented Jay. 'There's no sight
quite like it on earth.'

Charlie was definitely ready to agree with that! She
strongly suspected, though, that she and Jay were looking
at it from very different points of view.

'How on earth are we going to land?' she asked
uneasily. 'There isn't a square inch of space down there.'

'There's a small landing-strip a little further on,' he
explained. 'It was built several years ago by an oil
company who were prospecting in the area. They soon
abandoned the project, though. Now, the landing-strip's
used mainly by missionaries, who fly in every so often
to give the Indians a medical check-up. This particular
tribe that Jim's been studying have set up camp in a
clearing right next to the air-strip, which is lucky for us.
A long walk through the jungle is no joke, no matter
how fit you are, or how well equipped. In fact, I wouldn't

27

have brought you with me if we hadn't been staying close to the air-strip. And, of course, Jim's got a radio. If anything goes wrong, we can just call for help, and they'll have us out of there in no time.'

Charlie looked at him guardedly. 'What's likely to go wrong?'

'Nothing, as long as we're sensible and careful. But this won't be like a camping holiday back home,' he warned. 'It's pretty primitive down there.'

She grimaced. 'I'm still trying to work out how you managed to talk me into coming along with you.'

'It was your suggestion,' he reminded her.

'But I didn't mean it!' she protested. 'And I certainly never thought you'd take it seriously. No one takes a secretary along with them on a trip to the jungle, so they can sit and write a novel in their spare time!'

Jay laughed. 'I'm afraid I've never been very conventional,' he admitted. 'Anyway, I'm used to working in unusual circumstances; I won't have any problems concentrating on the book. And I really would like to get it finished. Once I've started something, I like to see it through to the end.'

Since Charlie had suspected all along that he was capable of being almost frighteningly single-minded, she wasn't very surprised by that particular admission. And, despite her attempts at light-heartedness, she knew she wasn't looking forward to the prospect of spending the next three or four weeks in his company. It wouldn't be like working in that comfortable house of his on the south coast, where she could just walk out, get into her car and drive away if things got too awkward or difficult. Here, she would be trapped. There was no way out, except by plane, and the pilot would only make an unscheduled flight here in a real emergency. He wouldn't obligingly drop in and pick her up just because she and Jay weren't getting on too well together!

Not that there was any reason to suspect there was going to be any friction between them. On the surface at least, Jay seemed to have a totally relaxed attitude to life. In the short time they had been together, she had found him surprisingly easy to get along with, and he had shown absolutely no inclination to pry into her private life once he had realised that it was a subject she didn't want to talk about.

So why did she still keep feeling so edgy? Perhaps it was because she suspected that a sharply inquisitive brain lurked behind that laid-back attitude; that it was just a front he deliberately used to put people at ease, to lower their defences. He would wait for that moment when their guard was down completely, leaving them totally vulnerable; then he would jump in and take them apart at leisure, knowing that they wouldn't be able to resist his gentle but thorough probing into the very depths of their minds.

Despite the humid heat, Charlie shivered. Stop being fanciful, she ordered herself with some annoyance. It was no use letting her nerves get out of hand before this trip even got properly under way.

She turned away from Jay and stared out of the window again. Then her gaze fixed on something below and she peered even harder. 'Is that the landing-strip?' she asked a few moments later.

'It looks like it,' agreed Jay. 'We should be back on the ground in just a few minutes.'

The pilot circled round the strip, then finally set the plane down with more enthusiasm than skill. Charlie glanced anxiously towards the small bag that held her photographic equipment, all of it on loan from the magazine's photographic department. If either of the expensive cameras had been damaged, Dan most definitely wouldn't be pleased. He was relying on her to get some good shots that he could use in conjunction with

her feature. Since she was strictly an amateur pho-
tographer, he had loaded her up with a massive supply
of film and instructed her to shoot anything that moved.
'With a lot of luck, we might just end up with half a
dozen pictures we can use,' he had told her.

The plane finally jolted its way to a halt. Charlie
scrambled out, and as Jay and the pilot began to unload
the supplies they had brought with them, she stared
around her with some trepidation. On the far side of
the landing-strip flowed a wide, sluggish moving river.
She couldn't see any further than that because of the
tall, green curtain of trees. There were more trees behind
her, and though she was ready to admit that they had a
certain presence, almost a magnificence, she strongly
suspected that she was going to get very sick of the sight
of them before her stay here was finally over.

It didn't take the two men long to unload the plane;
then the pilot gave them a grin and a brief wave. 'I'll
be back in three weeks,' he told them. 'If anything goes
wrong before then just radio for help and I'll come and
pick you up. It's got to be a real emergency, though. I
won't be dropping in just because you've run out of sugar
or want an aspirin for a headache!'

Jay shook hands with him, and minutes later the plane
took off and buzzed off out of sight. For a while, Charlie
simply stood and watched it disappearing into the distance. A queer feeling of panic had begun to cramp her
stomach. She wanted to jump up and down and wave
her arms, anything that would get the plane to turn round
and take her back to civilisation.

'Just realising what you've let yourself in for?' asked
Jay perceptively.

She swallowed hard, and tried to ignore her wildly
fluttering nerves. 'I didn't think it would feel quite so—
so isolated,' she admitted. 'But I can cope,' she added
quickly. And she stubbornly told herself she was telling

the truth, she *could* cope. She was going to get through the next three or four weeks, and come out of it with a story so good that it would make Dan's eyes pop out when he read it!

Firmly, she picked up her large shoulder-bag and looked around. 'Where's this hut we're meant to be staying in?'

They were going to live in the hut that had been Jim Fielding's home for the past few months, while he had carried out his extensive study of the tribe of Indians who regarded this stretch of rain forest as their territory. Jay had told her that the Indians themselves shared a couple of huts close by, living in large family groups, children, parents, grandparents and even great-grandparents all living amicably under the same roof.

Jay glanced towards the end of the landing-strip. 'Jim said the huts were in a small clearing just beyond the runway,' he told her. 'They shouldn't be too hard to find.'

'I don't remember seeing them as we flew in, even though I was looking out for them,' Charlie remarked a little uneasily. 'Are you sure we're in the right place?'

Jay lifted one eyebrow expressively. 'How many landing-strips do you suppose there are in the middle of this stretch of rain forest?'

'All right, there's no need to sound so superior!' she retorted crossly. 'Let's go and find this hut before it starts to rain.'

The sky definitely looked rather ominous, with heavy, low cloud closing in all round them. Charlie guessed that they didn't call this a rain forest for nothing, and that she was going to have to get used to getting regularly drenched. Even when the rain stopped and the sun blazed down, the high humidity would still make everything seem damp. She didn't intend to let a little thing like adverse weather conditions get her down, though. She was here to get a story, and that was precisely what she was going to end up with, a humdinger of an article that would grab the readers by the throat and force them to read every single word.

She trudged determinedly off after Jay as he strode along the landing-strip. When they reached the end, she could just about make out a faint path that led through a narrow belt of trees. Jay had seen it, too, and he immediately began to follow it.

A couple of minutes later, the trees thinned out again. They found themselves entering a small clearing, which was empty except for three large mounds of what looked like long branches and dead leaves. One was fairly close to them, the other two on the far side of the clearing. Charlie supposed it was the rubbish that had been left over after the landing-strip had been cleared, dumped here to rot away, and she didn't take any further notice.

Jay, though, was nodding with satisfaction. 'At least it didn't take us too long to find the huts.'

Charlie swung round to face him with a puzzled frown. 'Huts? What huts? Where are they?'

'Either you need glasses, or you're about to get an unpleasant shock,' he told her drily. 'You're standing just a few yards in front of one.'

Her gaze drifted back in disbelief to the nearest mound of branches and leaves. In size and shape, it looked rather like a very old hayrick, and she blinked very hard. 'That's a *hut*?'

Jay was grinning openly now. 'What were you expecting? A two up, two down, with running water and central heating?'

'No, of course not,' said Charlie indignantly. 'I just thought——' Her voice trailed away. No wonder she hadn't been able to spot any huts from the plane! She had been looking for a prefab type of building, nothing fancy—and certainly nothing like Jay's slightly sarcastic description—but something with four recognisable walls, and perhaps a corrugated roof to keep the rain out. He didn't seriously expect her to spend the next couple of weeks living under a heap of dead leaves?

Apparently he did, because he was already walking towards it.

'This is definitely Jim's hut,' he confirmed a moment later, with another grin. 'Look!'

Hanging over a large gap in the leaves that, by stretching her imagination to the limit, she could just about recognise as a doorway, was a roughly made wooden sign with some letters inexpertly etched on to it.

'"Home sweet home",' she read, her eyebrows shooting up as far as they could possibly go. 'Your friend's got a very weird sense of humour!'

'He also likes to live fairly comfortably when he's away on these long field trips,' Jay told her. 'It's probably far more cosy inside than you'd think.'

But Charlie was still in an advanced state of shock. Numbly, she followed him through the open doorway, wondering how many more surprises she was going to encounter before the day was over—and if her nervous system was going to prove capable of coping with them without collapsing completely!

Inside, it was dark and shadowy, although far larger than she had expected. From the outside, the size was definitely deceptive. Although she couldn't see clearly, she had the impression that the roof was fourteen or fifteen feet high, and the hut itself must have been nearly twenty by twenty.

Not that that made things any better. She was just about to declare that she couldn't possibly live here, then turn round and stalk out, when it hit her rather forcibly that she didn't have a lot of choice. Short of sleeping out in the open—and she had enough common sense to realise that that definitely *wasn't* a practical or desirable proposition—this was the only alternative.

Jay had dug around in his own bag, and now he brought out a torch. Flicking on its powerful beam, he let the light slowly trace a path around the interior of the hut, resting every now and then on different items. Charlie soon realised that the back of the hut had been set aside as a sleeping area, with a large hammock slung between two of the thick crossbeams. The rest of the hut had been roughly divided into half. One was an eating and cooking area, with a small folding table and chairs, a two-ring camping stove and boxes of supplies. The other half looked like a working area. It even had a small filing cabinet, and it was much more well organised than the rest of the hut.

After slinging his bag down on to the floor, Jay glanced at his watch. 'We'd better get the rest of our supplies stowed away. There's only another couple of hours of daylight left—it gets dark around half-past six. Are you going to lend a hand, or are you going to stand around for the rest of the day, complaining?'

'Of course I'll give you a hand,' replied Charlie with some dignity. 'And I wasn't complaining, it's just that it's not—well, not quite what I was expecting.'

'I warned you it would be primitive,' he reminded her.

And so he had, during those frantically busy days before they had actually left. But, for some reason, she had closed her mind to what he had been telling her. All she had been concentrating on was getting her story, already plotting out possible outlines in her mind, working out how she could use this trip to give it a really exotic background.

'There's primitive and there's *primitive*,' she now muttered darkly. 'And then there's this—which is something else again!'

But Jay didn't seem to be listening to her. In fact, now she came to think about it, she realised he had seemed slightly preoccupied ever since they had got off the plane. He turned and went out of the hut, then just stood outside, staring around him with a definite frown on his face.

Charlie went to stand beside him. 'What's the matter?' she asked curiously.

'What can you see?'

That wasn't a difficult question to answer. 'Trees,' she told him promptly.

'And what can you hear?'

She stopped for a couple of seconds to think about that one. 'Insects,' she answered finally. 'They're buzzing around all over the place. Oh, and those beautiful blue and gold birds that keep swooping around overhead and squawking like mad.'

'Macaws,' he told her, slightly absently.

'What *should* I be seeing and hearing?'

He shot her a faintly exasperated glance, both his blue eye and his green eye looking at her as if they hadn't expected to find her so simple-minded.

'Indians,' he replied succinctly. 'The minute the plane landed, they should have come out to meet us. The arrival of a plane's always a big event in their lives. They should be living in those huts over there.' He gestured to the huts on the far side of the clearing. 'The children should be playing outside, the men and women either lazing around in hammocks or getting on with their everyday chores. So—where are they?'

Charlie shrugged philosophically. 'At a guess, I'd say they weren't here,' she responded, not very helpfully.

For a moment, those odd eyes flickered with bright impatience, and a small shiver rippled uncomfortably down her spine. She had been right; that casual, relaxed attitude was just a front. Underneath lurked a very different kind of man, one who was quick, alert, possibly frighteningly perceptive—and who definitely didn't suffer fools gladly.

To her relief, though, he seemed to have decided to simply ignore her rather inane remark. Instead, he set off towards the landing-strip, intent on getting all their supplies under cover before darkness fell. By the time Charlie had huffed and puffed her way to the landing-strip and back half a dozen times, toting some of the lighter boxes, she felt dead beat. She knew it was partly due to the amount of travelling she had done over the last couple of days, and also to the high humidity, which seemed to be sapping all the energy from her bones and muscles.

Staggering back to the hut for the last time, she dumped her box on the ground, then sat on it.

'I vote we have something to eat, then an early night. I've just about had it. I could sleep a week!'

'Do you want to tackle the camping stove yourself, or do you want me to rustle up some food?'

She stared at him in surprise. 'You can cook?'

He shot her a dry look. 'I've been on field trips before,' he reminded her. 'And, since there are rarely any females around, you soon learn to cook, or you get very hungry.'

'You had a woman with you on both of your last trips,' she reminded him, slightly tartly.

'So I did,' he agreed, his gaze returning to her and fixing on her thoughtfully. 'You sound as if you thoroughly disapprove. Do you think I should have gone on my own?'

Charlie very nearly told him exactly what she thought; that he had had no right to drag those girls off to remote corners of the world just so he could write a book about the whole experience and make a lot of money out of it; that he had just been *using* them. At the last moment, though, she forced herself to stay silent. There was no point in provoking him into a heated argument. Anyway, she was too tired to think straight right now. This was something she would prefer to discuss with him when she was fully awake and alert. She had already decided this could well make a good basis for her article: whether someone had a moral right to use another person for their own purposes.

'We'll talk about it some other time,' she hedged. 'Right at this moment, I just want something to eat. And, since you're so domesticated, you can definitely tackle the cooking.'

'It won't be anything fancy,' he warned. 'Just something warmed up out of a tin.'

But Charlie was beyond caring. She simply wanted to shovel something into her empty stomach, then curl up and go to sleep.

It was getting dark now, so Jay dug out some candles from the boxful they had brought with them. He fixed them in their holders, then lit them.

'Very romantic,' murmured Charlie. 'Where are the violins?'

Jay grinned. 'I'm tone deaf—I can't even whistle in tune! If you want music, you'll have to provide it yourself.'

In a remarkably short time, there was a plate of hot food in front of her. As Jay had warned, it was a simple meal, just tinned meat and vegetables, but Charlie ate it with relish. Then she sat back and sighed with satisfaction.

'Fantastic. Now, if you don't mind, I'm going to climb straight into that hammock. If I don't go to bed, I'm going to fall asleep right here, in this chair.'

'Actually, that's *my* hammock,' Jay remarked casually. 'I've brought a newer, more comfortable one for you. It's still packed away in one of the boxes. Just give me a few minutes, and I'll get it out and fix it up for you.'

Charlie suddenly didn't feel nearly as sleepy as she had only seconds before. She sat up very straight and stared at him guardedly.

'Just where are you planning to fix this hammock?'

'Right alongside mine, of course,' he told her calmly. 'We don't really have any option, it's got to be fixed to the crossbeams.'

'But I thought——' she began rather nervously.

Jay's eyes narrowed perceptibly. 'You thought what?'

'Well—that you'd be sleeping in one of the other huts.'

'What made you think that?' His voice was still perfectly calm, so Charlie couldn't work out why she suddenly felt so horribly edgy.

'It seemed fairly obvious,' she blustered.

'It's not at all obvious to me,' he told her, and this time there was a new and distinct note of coolness in his voice. Charlie wriggled uncomfortably on her chair. All the same, she didn't intend to give in over this. Worming her way into his life so she could get a story on him was one thing, but this was something else. It was going to be bad enough spending practically every waking hour in his company, but with luck she could just about cope with that. She definitely didn't intend to sleep right beside him, though!

'If you won't sleep in one of the other huts, I will,' she informed him firmly. 'If you'd just be kind enough to fix up my hammock——'

In two strides, he was standing beside her and looming over her. Charlie gulped audibly. She hadn't even seen him move! For a big man, he could move with deadly speed, like some huge cat at the peak of its hunting powers.

'Since you don't strike me as someone who's simple-minded, I'll put this childish attitude of yours down to sheer tiredness,' came his slightly grim response. 'Do you seriously think I'd let you sleep on your own? What do you think this is, some damned holiday camp? Use your head, Charlotte!'

It always set her nerves totally on edge when he used her full name. A lot of deeply buried memories rushed straight to the surface and threatened to tear her apart all over again.

'Don't call me that!' she said furiously. 'And don't accuse me of being childish. That's one thing I'm definitely not, and haven't been for years. Anyway, why are you making all this fuss? Just because I don't want to sleep with you——'

'I'm not asking you to sleep *with* me,' he cut in irritably. 'You're here to work, not have a good time.'

At that, her eyebrows shot sky-high with incredulity.

'*A good time?*' she flung back at him in disbelief. 'My God, you've got a high opinion of yourself! Is that what you really think?' she went on with growing sarcasm. 'That a woman's only got to climb into your bed and the earth begins to shake?'

Those strange-coloured eyes of his glittered furiously for a few seconds. Then, without warning, the anger completely vanished and in its place came a spark of bright amusement.

'I've never had any complaints,' Jay told her, his voice relaxing into a lazy drawl. 'But how on earth did we get on to this ridiculous subject? I don't suppose you're any more interested in my sex-life than I am in yours. Though if the way you over-reacted is anything to go by, I'd guess that yours hasn't been running too smoothly lately.' Catching the quick flare of hostility that swept over her face, he went on immediately, 'That's no business of mine, though. All I'm concerned about is making sure that you stay perfectly safe while you're working for me. You're in an environment that you know virtually nothing about, so it makes sense for you to stick close to me while you're here. And that includes the nights, as well as the days. If you're really so prudish that the sight of my body's going to make you blush, I'll fix up a couple of blankets between the hammocks, so you'll have some privacy.'

'Thank you,' muttered Charlie, knowing that this was the best offer she was going to get from him, and she had better grab it.

It didn't take him long to fix the hammock into place. Then he tied a length of rope right across the hut, and draped a couple of blankets over it to form a makeshift curtain.

'Goodnight,' Charlie said stiffly. She grabbed a candle, then retreated behind the curtain with as much dignity as she could muster.

The hammock was surprisingly comfortable once she had managed to clamber into it. She was a little hot inside the sleeping-bag, but Jay had warned her it would get quite chilly towards dawn. Although the temperature rarely fell below seventy, even at night, the high humidity made it feel a lot cooler during the hours of darkness.

As she lay there, she could hear Jay moving around, sorting out their supplies. Even if he had been sitting still and not making a sound, she would still have known he was there. He was a man who seemed able to make his presence felt even though he couldn't be seen or heard.

Charlie moved restlessly, trying to force her tired muscles to relax. When she had set out on this trip, she hadn't let herself think too hard about the obvious problems that would crop up, living so close to Jay Challoner for three or four weeks. She had been only too aware that they existed—at least, for her they certainly did—but she had fiercely told herself that she could cope, that she *had* to cope if she wanted to get this story. But now look what had happened: the first little obstacle, a silly thing like the two of them sleeping in the same hut, and she had nearly blown the whole thing by wildly over-reacting.

She clenched her teeth and told herself she wouldn't let it happen again. If there was one lesson she had learnt during these last three years, it was how to control her nerves. It was either that, and beginning to live a relatively normal life again, or letting herself go under completely. And, despite everything that had happened, she hadn't quite lost her fighting spirit. Somehow she had survived all the traumas, moved down to London, got herself a job and a flat, hauled herself back into the real world again. She didn't intend to throw all that effort away just because she was having problems adjusting to living temporarily with a man.

No, not just a man, she reminded herself. Jay Challoner, who could give her career a real boost if she could ferret out enough material for a first-class feature. And she wouldn't let herself feel any qualms about the way she was going about getting that information. She was still strongly of the opinion that he had simply used those women he had featured in his two best-selling books. Well, now it was her turn to use him. If he didn't like it, that was too bad. Anyway, he wouldn't find out about it until it was too late, and her article had been published.

A gust of wind made the walls of the hut rustle and vibrate, and Charlie closed her eyes, trying to ignore her surroundings. Minutes later, rain began to teem down, hissing loudly as it hit the leaves. The sound seemed to get right inside her head, echoing round and round inside it until she gritted her teeth and wanted to yell at it to stop.

Miraculously, it did. Charlie sighed with relief, and tried to convince herself that a couple of weeks of living in this awful place wasn't going to drive her right out of her mind. Then she decided she had better get to sleep before the rain started up again. Just minutes later, she was dead to the world, and slept like a log for the rest of the night.

CHAPTER THREE

NEXT morning, Charlie poked her head out through the open doorway at the front of the hut, then gave a beam of pure delight. The rain forest had been miraculously transformed from the depressing, drenched place it had seemed last night, just before she had gone to sleep. The sun was shining brilliantly out of a clear blue sky, bees were droning about busily, the gorgeously coloured macaws were noisily flapping around overhead, while from the sun-splashed trees all around came noisy bursts of squawks and clucks as dozens of unseen and un-identifiable birds enthusiastically greeted the new day.

Charlie stood there for a while, soaking up the warm sunshine and enjoying the discordant bird songs. Then she saw Jay walking across the clearing towards the hut, toting a couple of large buckets.

'We can't run to a bath, I'm afraid,' he said cheer-fully, plonking down the buckets. 'You'll have to make do with a quick wash-down.'

'Can't I just go and dunk myself in the river?' suggested Charlie.

'Only if I come with you. Remember what I told you last night,' he reminded her. 'Stick close to me at all times. I'm responsible for your safety while you're here, and I don't intend to let anything happen to you.'

'Like what?' she said cautiously.

Jay shrugged. 'Snakes can be a problem, if you don't keep your eyes open. Several of the insects can give a nasty bite, and then there's always the chance of meeting up with a jaguar.' Seeing her eyes open wide with alarm, he added, 'Don't worry, we've got a comprehensive medical kit, including a treatment for snakebite. And Jim told me he hadn't seen any sign of a big cat during all the time he was here.'

Charlie grimaced, then peered into the nearest bucket of water. A moment later, she wrinkled her nose.

'It doesn't look very—well, clean,' she said fastidiously.

Jay grinned. 'Not quite the colour you're used to?' He glanced down at the muddy water. 'Jim's fixed up a rather ingenious filter system, if you want it to look clearer. It won't hurt you, though. The water's surprisingly fresh and clean, despite its colour. Anyway, by this time tomorrow you should be able to take a long, hot bath, if that's what you're hankering after.'

Charlie's head came up and she stared at him in surprise. 'What on earth do you mean?'

'There's not much point in sticking around now the Indians have gone. I can't study and make notes on a tribe that isn't even here.'

'But shouldn't you stay here, in case they come back?'

Jay shook his head. 'They won't be back. The Indians clear and cultivate small patches of forest, then plant manioc, which is a sort of root crop. Once one site's exhausted, they move on to a new one. The soil's so poor that you can't grow more than one crop on it; that's why they have to keep moving on and clearing fresh areas. That's obviously what's happened here, and it means they won't be returning to this particular spot.'

She lifted her eyebrows. 'You mean, we've come all this way for nothing?'

'It looks like it,' agreed Jay.

'But if the Indians have moved on, shouldn't we try and find them?'

'We'd get lost after we'd gone a dozen yards into that forest. It would be crazy even to try it. Jim's going to be pretty depressed when he hears what's happened, but there's nothing I can do about it. It means he's going to have to find the Indians again before he can even begin to pick up his study on them. And that won't be easy. Still, that'll be his problem. I feel sorry for the guy, but I've done all I can. There's nothing left to do now except radio the pilot and ask him if he can pick us up, and fly us out of here.'

Charlie felt an unexpected sense of deflation. Last night, feeling upset and depressed, she had gone to sleep wishing that someone would wave a magic wand and whisk her right out of this place. This morning, though, with the sun filtering through the trees and splashing the ground with bright patterns of colour, and the birds yelling their heads off in a marvellously tuneless cacophony, everything somehow seemed very different. Now that it looked as if she were about to get her wish and get out of here, she found herself not quite so eager to leave as she had thought she was.

All the same, she told herself, she definitely wouldn't mind sleeping in a proper bed again. Hammocks were all very well, but one sudden movement in the wrong direction could bring you down to earth, quite literally. And she had never before properly appreciated the comforts of modern plumbing. It wasn't until you had to use a chemical toilet, hidden discreetly behind a sheet of tarpaulin, that you started to think longingly of all those bathrooms, large and small, basic or luxurious, that you had taken for granted all your life.

Eventually, she gave a philosophical shrug. 'I'll begin packing things up again while you get on the radio,' she told Jay.

Several minutes later, she was stacking tins of food into a wooden box when he strode over to her, a dark frown lining his forehead.

'The radio's dead!' he announced in a grim tone.

Charlie stood very still. 'Dead?' she repeated apprehensively. 'What exactly do you mean—dead?'

A familiar flicker of impatience brightened Jay's eyes. 'It would be hard to put it any clearer. Dead—as in not working, no sound coming out of it, the whole bloody thing's useless.'

She looked at him guardedly. 'What's wrong with it? Can't you fix it?'

'I'm an anthropologist, not an electrician,' he reminded her in a low growl.

Charlie stared at him edgily. Coming here willingly, knowing that someone would fly in and whisk you out at the first hint of trouble, was one thing. Being stuck here, with no possible means of escape, and no contact with the outside world—well, that was something else again. And she didn't like it. She most definitely didn't like it! The first quiverings of panic were already beginning to flutter in the pit of her stomach.

'You—you've got to do something,' she stammered irrationally, as the feeling of being trapped swept over her in increasingly strong waves. 'You brought me here, you keep telling me you're responsible for me—so now you'd better find a way of getting me out of here!'

'Don't you think I would, if I could?' Jay retorted, the frustration clear in his voice. He swung round and prowled restlessly away from her. 'Jim told me the radio was in good working order. If I'd thought otherwise, I'd have brought a spare set with us.'

'I'm getting a bit tired of hearing what Jim said!' she snapped back at him. 'Jim told you the Indians would be here, but they weren't, we came all this way for nothing. Jim said we could use his hut, that we'd be quite comfortable, yet we're living like a couple of dropouts. And now the radio's not working, so we can't even get out of here. Do you suppose Jim's left any other little surprises that we haven't found out about yet?' she enquired sarcastically.

'This kind of attitude isn't going to help the situation,' Jay warned evenly.

'Then what exactly *is* going to help? We're stuck here, and yet you're just standing there, telling me that I've got the wrong attitude!'

'We're not in any immediate danger,' he reminded her. 'And the pilot's due to make his routine call in three weeks. All we've got to do is sit it out until then. We've got plenty of supplies, we certainly won't starve. I'll admit the hut's a bit primitive, but it'll give us all the shelter we need. And we were originally planning on staying for that length of time, anyway.'

'Yes, I know, but somehow it's different now we know that we don't *have* to stay. We can go home—except we can't,' Charlie said glumly.

'I've been in far worse places,' said Jay, beginning to sound unexpectedly cheerful again. By now, Charlie was coming to realise that his flashes of temper and irritability rarely lasted long, that he wasn't a moody man. 'Jim said that on a good day this could seem like the Garden of Eden.'

'If I remember rightly, that had snakes, too,' remarked Charlie with a fresh burst of gloominess. 'And if you mention your dear friend Jim again, I might well scream—very loudly!'

'Then let's make an effort to be more positive about the whole situation,' Jay suggested. 'It might be a good idea to begin by drawing up some kind of work schedule——'

'Work?' squeaked Charlie.

Jay looked faintly surprised. 'Why not? It's the reason I brought you here, remember? And now we'll have three undisturbed weeks to get on with the book. This could all work out very well,' he went on with growing enthusiasm. 'I could get the bulk of the book finished in that time.'

'I don't believe I'm hearing this,' she muttered. 'Here we are, stranded in the middle of the rain forest, and you're talking about work schedules! You're behaving as if all of this is perfectly normal, something that happens every day.'

His dark brows twitched with fresh impatience. 'I'm simply saying that we might as well make the most of this opportunity. I don't intend to sit around and do nothing for the next three weeks. I like to relax, but I certainly don't enjoy being idle. And I shouldn't think you'd find it much fun, either. You'd be bored to death after a couple of days. So why not make good use of the time, and get on with the book?'

'It's all very well for you,' Charlie retorted. 'Considering your track record, you're probably quite used to working in all sorts of unusual places and situations. I normally work in an office, though—a comfortable place with four walls, a window, and a lot of useful electronic equipment. Believe it or not, I'm not used to sitting in the middle of the jungle and taking dictation!'

His gaze rested on her with new coolness. 'Then why did you agree to come? I explained precisely what you would be letting yourself in for, I told you the sort of conditions you'd be living and working under. To be honest, I expected you to turn me down flat. Most girls would have bolted straight out the door the moment I suggested it. You didn't, though. Why, Charlotte?'

It was a question that she wouldn't—couldn't—answer truthfully. If she told him the truth—that her editor had told her to stick to Jay Challoner like glue, no matter where he went—then that would finish any chance she had ever had of getting a story.

So, instead, she smiled rather feebly and scraped around inside her head for an explanation that would sound feasible.

'I told you, I admire your books,' she said at last. 'I wanted to have the chance to work for you. When you suggested this trip, I thought it would be—well, a challenge,' she waffled on, wondering if he was swallowing a single word of this. 'I'm sorry if I've not been behaving very well,' she finished contritely, gazing up at him with her most innocent expression. 'I'll try to be more mature in future. And I'll work hard, I promise I will. Between the two of us, we'll get this new book of yours finished in record time.'

But Jay was staring down at her now with a distinctly speculative expression on his face. For some reason, she didn't like—or trust—that look, it made it too hard to guess what he was really thinking. It wasn't too long, though, before she found out exactly what was going through his head.

'I wonder how many men have stared straight into those big blue eyes of yours, and swallowed every word you've told them?' he mused, his dark brows drawing together thoughtfully.

Charlie gazed back at him with the beginnings of apprehension. 'I don't think I know what you mean.'

He smiled, a dry twist of his lips which somehow managed to make her feel thoroughly uncomfortable.

'Come on, Charlotte,' came his gentle response, 'I get the feeling that you know exactly what I mean. Those huge eyes of yours are as much of an asset as that gorgeous blonde hair. No woman in her right mind would fail to make use of physical advantages like those.'

'That's not a very nice thing to say—it makes me sound scheming and conniving,' she retorted with some annoyance, conveniently forgetting all the times she had batted her blue eyes at some man and ended up getting precisely what she wanted.

'I'm not sure yet what you are,' Jay replied. His gaze was still fixed on her with a disturbing, unwavering quality, as if this was a problem he had suddenly become very interested in solving.

Deeply uneasy, for no real reason that she could put her finger on, Charlie pointedly turned her back on him, clearly signalling that this conversation was at an end as far as she was concerned. Then she busied herself with tidying away some tins of food that had been left lying around. She had no intention of letting Jay Challoner poke around inside her head, uncovering all her carefully guarded secrets. And, to her relief, he didn't attempt to probe any further.

For the rest of the day, they set about getting their temporary home into some kind of order. Jay explained the mysteries of the camping stove to Charlie, so that she finally felt confident she could produce a hot meal, even though it might not be up to cordon bleu standards. All the food they had brought with them was either tinned or dried, since anything fresh would quickly rot in the hot, humid atmosphere. Jay reckoned he could catch fish from the river to supplement what was going to be a fairly monotonous diet, and the forest would provide them with a certain amount of fresh fruit.

The next morning, they started work. To begin with, Charlie found it distinctly bizarre, sitting and taking dictation in this exotic setting. She got used to it surprisingly quickly, though, and soon learnt how to shut out the distracting sounds and colours all around her.

One thing became obvious almost straight away. Jay Challoner certainly knew how to work hard! He dictated fast and fluently, so that the first chapters began to take shape with amazing speed. Charlie realised that he must have the whole novel mapped out inside his head;

it was just a question of getting it down on paper. Although she didn't usually go for thrillers, she was enjoying this one immensely. The fast, pacy plot and crisp dialogue made the book race along at tremendous speed. She was already getting impatient to know how it was finally going to end.

She had set up the folding table and chair in the doorway of the hut, where there was a good light, but she was shaded from the full brilliance of the sunshine. The portable typewriter clacked away as she transcribed the pages of shorthand, the sound echoing round the clearing, out of place in this primitive setting, and yet somehow blending in with all the other background noises. When clouds swept across the blue sky and heavy bursts of rain drenched the clearing, as happened regularly, she simply moved the table and chair back inside the hut; then she waited until the skies cleared again.

After a couple of days, she began to congratulate herself on the way things were going. It was all working out far better than she had dared hope. There hadn't been any major problems, and it looked as if the two and a half weeks still to go before the plane returned were going to be surprisingly easy to get through. She had got up early that morning so she could get in a couple of hours' work before it got too hot, and she looked at the heap of neatly typed pages with some satisfaction. And in a folder that was carefully hidden away, there were some more typed pages—the notes that would, she hoped, form the basis of her article. She had forced herself to begin work on them because she had been a little alarmed to find that it was beginning to get more and more difficult to remember why she was really here. Being so isolated, so cut off from the outside world, was making her feel oddly distant from the busy life she led in London. She didn't really like that, she had the feeling it could be dangerous to let herself slip into that frame of mind. This was only an illusion of paradise, she reminded herself more than once, not paradise itself. She had better remember that, or she could end up in a whole lot of trouble.

Jay crossed the clearing at that point, interrupting her wandering thoughts. He had also been up early this morning, borrowing the fishing-rod Jim had left behind, and going down to the river to try his luck.

Charlie looked unenthusiastically at the fish he was carrying. 'I hope you don't expect me to clean and gut them,' she said with a dark grimace.

'Squeamish?' he mocked gently. Then he relented. 'Don't worry, you won't have to touch them until they're neatly cut up and ready for the pan. I'll even cook them, if you like.'

'Good,' she said, with some relief. Then she added, 'Are you going to clean them right now, or do you want to get on with some more dictation first?'

He put down the fish and the rod, then came over and stood in front of her. She could never relax when he was this close, he always seemed to loom over her, he was so big, so—well, perhaps threatening wasn't quite the right word, but something inside her always started to quiver when he stood so near.

'Before either of us do anything else, there's one important thing we ought to take care of,' he told her, after a slight pause.

'What?' she asked, slightly guardedly.

'The main problem around here is insects. They can be a real problem.'

'I know that,' came her rather rueful reply. She already had half a dozen itchy bites, although she had found some tubes of cream in their medical kit that had stopped the worst of the irritation.

Jay frowned lightly. 'I'm talking about parasites, not insects that bite and then fly away.'

'Parasites?' echoed Charlie, with a touch of distaste.

'They can burrow right under the skin,' he warned. 'If you don't dig them out fairly quickly, infection can set in and the whole area can get very painful.'

'Oh, great!' she said gloomily. 'Just when you think you're getting used to this place, and even starting to like it, something really nasty pops up to spoil it.'

'These parasites needn't be a problem,' Jay said re-assuringly. 'It's just a question of regularly checking yourself from head to foot, making sure that you haven't got any patches of skin that are red or inflamed.'

'I'm not a contortionist,' she reminded him a little acidly. 'The front won't cause any problems, but the only way I can see my back is with a full-length mirror. And I don't remember seeing any of those lying around.'

Jay looked at her calmly. 'That's why we'll have to check each other.'

It took a few seconds for the full implication of that remark to sink in. When it did, Charlie lifted her head and let him see the cold expression on her face.

'That won't be necessary,' came her frosty response. 'I'll find some way of getting round the problem. I won't need any help from you.'

Jay shook his head. 'It can't be done. You don't need just your back checked, but the whole of your scalp as well. It can only be done thoroughly if someone else does it for you.'

'In that case, we'll just scrap the whole idea,' she shot back instantly. 'I don't mind taking my chances with a few parasites.'

'But I *do* mind. Very much,' he told her evenly. 'I intend to make sure that you leave this place as healthy as when you arrived.'

Her stomach had begun to churn now, and her pulse rate had practically doubled. She was still sure she could get out of it, though. After all, he couldn't force her to

subject herself to a body-search. Then she glanced up
at him, and a fresh rush of doubt surged over her. He
probably *could* force her, she realised edgily. He was
certainly big enough. And those were muscles under the
thin cotton of his shirt, not flab. If he was really determined to go through with this——

Her limbs had already started to stiffen, and she knew
that soon they would be almost frozen with tension. Jay
didn't seem to realise that anything was wrong, though.
He had gone into the hut, but reappeared, only moments later, carrying a blanket. He spread it out on a
clear patch of ground in front of the hut, then turned
back to Charlie.

'Do you want to go first, or shall I?' She didn't—
couldn't—answer, and Jay gave a brief sigh of impatience; then he began to strip off his shirt. Charlie
instantly looked away, and he stopped undressing, a definite frown darkening his face now.

'Look, this isn't some game,' he told her, a distinct
edge very noticeable in his voice. 'This is vital to our
good health. I've no idea why you're putting on this
ridiculous display of prudishness, but if it'll make you
any happier—and more co-operative—let's get a couple
of things straight. You think I'm going to jump on you
the moment you're undressed? I'm not. It's a long time
since I was a raw adolescent. You might at least credit
me with a certain amount of self-control.' His gaze fixed
on her even more searchingly, and he seemed to realise
that she still wasn't convinced. 'What is it?' he went on
in a slightly puzzled tone. 'Are you nervous because
there's just the two of us? That there's no one to come
rushing to help you if the situation gets out of hand?
But it won't get out of hand,' he promised. 'I'm not
doing this for the fun of seeing you half-naked. I certainly don't need to get my kicks that way.'

That, at least, Charlie could believe. Although there was no way she could ever be interested in him herself, she could look at him quite detachedly and see that most women would go weak-kneed at just the sight of him. Odd, really, because he wasn't good-looking in the conventional sense. His features were—striking, she decided after a moment's thought. And strong, very strong. And those bi-coloured eyes, lined with thick lashes and half-shadowed by the eyebrows that could move so expressively—they were all part of the man's formidable armoury of charm.

As he quickly and easily began to step out of the rest of his clothes, Charlie could see that the rest of him matched the promise of that unusual face. He was big, yet not thickset, his shoulders powerful, his waist and hips perfectly in proportion. No wonder he had been flooded with applications from girls who had wanted to scoot off to Africa with him for several months! If things had been different, she might have been tempted to post off one of those applications herself.

But things weren't different, she reminded herself as reality came thundering back again, taking the edge of brightness off the morning. And she was unshakably certain that they never would be different, no matter what might happen to her in the future.

First, though, she had to cope with the present. To her relief, Jay had stopped just short of total nakedness, although the cotton briefs he was wearing really didn't make much difference. They barely covered his well formed body, and certainly left very little to the imagination. Seconds later, he lay down on his stomach; then he turned his head slightly, so he could look up at her.

'You'd better check the backs of my thighs and arms, my back itself, my neck, then my scalp. It shouldn't take more than a couple of minutes. If you see any areas that look red or sore, give a yell.'

With grim reluctance, Charlie slowly knelt beside him on the blanket. Without touching him, she somehow managed to do a fairly comprehensive visual survey of his body. His skin was lightly tanned, and had a healthy silky sheen to it. It was also flawless, with no sign of any parasite infestation.

'No hands?' Jay remarked lightly, when she had finally finished peering at him. 'That was a clever trick, Charlotte. It won't work for the next bit, though. There's no way you can examine my scalp without touching my hair.'

But she had already realised that. With some distaste, she stared down at his dark, glossy hair. Then, with a deep breath, and using just the very tips of her fingers she gingerly reached out and began to part it. She concentrated hard on the clean, unmarked scalp beneath and forced herself to ignore the warm, soft brushing of the dark curls against her skin.

It seemed to take for ever, although common sense told her it couldn't have been more than three or four minutes. Finally, giving a huge sigh of relief, she snatched her hands away and sat back.

'There's not a mark on you anywhere,' she told him, her voice almost cheerful now the ordeal was over. 'Obviously parasites don't find you in the least attractive.'

'Apparently you don't, either,' he commented drily, as he sat up. 'All right, it's your turn now. Strip off and lie down.'

In her relief that she didn't have to touch him any more, she had momentarily forgotten that this was a two-way operation. All her old apprehension instantly rushed back, and she sat as still as a statue. She couldn't do it, she knew she couldn't. Her stomach was already churning with the first echoes of nausea.

'Charlotte, I'm getting tired of these games. Do as I say!' Jay ordered peremptorily.

To her astonishment, she found herself instantly obeying him. Seconds ago, she hadn't been able to move. Now, she was clambering out of her clothes; in just seconds she had stripped down to her plain cotton bra and pants. She kept her back to him during the entire operation, and as soon as she was undressed, she hurriedly stretched herself out on the blanket. She lay stomach downwards, then stared fixedly in front of her, so she wouldn't have to see him. She could still sense him leaning over her, though, so she knew the precise moment that his hands began to move towards her. Although she could predict exactly what her reaction was going to be the instant his fingertips came into contact with her shrinking skin, she also knew there wasn't a single thing she could do to stop it, no matter how hard she tried.

An instant later, Jay casually rested one hand on the small of her back—and it happened. She flinched wildly, her flesh actually drawing back from his touch, as if his fingertips had been coated with burning acid.

Jay's own sense of shock communicated itself to her, but his hands didn't move. 'All right, I get the message,' he said at last, with unexpected sympathy. 'But it's got to be done. Just keep still, and I'll be as quick as I can.'

With expert thoroughness, he checked her over, briefly pulling down her pants so he could inspect the firm swell of her buttocks, then undoing her bra strap and letting his gaze slide over the pale skin underneath. Finally, his fingers began to thread their way through the blonde strands of her hair. The sensation made her entire scalp crawl; she thought that if this went on for one second longer, she was actually going to scream out loud. Then, to her relief, it was over. No more touching, no more of that bright, piercing gaze raking over her skin. Jay had

settled back on his haunches, not moving now, his whole
body unnaturally still.

She couldn't get up, not while he was still sitting there.
She lay there, feeling utterly miserable and somehow
dirty, and wished he would just go away. If he left her
on her own for a while, she would eventually be all right
again. She would be able to blot this episode right out
of her mind, as she had succeeded in blotting out so
much else.

Jay stayed exactly where he was, though. His silence
unnerved her; she almost wished he would shout at her,
lose his temper, show some kind of reaction. In the end,
she couldn't stand it any longer. She turned her head
and glared at him in sudden anger.

'Well?' she demanded. 'Aren't you going to say something? Don't tell me you're dumbstruck for once!' she
added with heavy sarcasm.

'No, not dumbstruck,' he agreed quietly. 'But I'd be
lying if I said I wasn't surprised. On the surface, you're
bright, cheerful and outgoing. Several times I got the
impression that there was a whole lot more to you than
that, but I decided not to probe too deeply; I thought
it would be easier to take you at face value. After all,
you were only going to be working for me temporarily.
In a few weeks, we'd be going our separate ways, chances
were we'd never even meet again.'

She studied his face suspiciously. 'Why do you keep
talking in the past tense? Nothing's changed. We'll only
be working together for a short while, just the way you
said. Then we'll start leading our own lives again.
Everything will get back to normal.'

His eyes fixed on her searchingly. 'And exactly what
is normal for you, Charlotte?' he asked softly.

'What do you mean?' came her evasive mutter.

Jay's expression altered, hardening and darkening.
'Don't pretend to be stupid or naive,' he warned. 'You're

very obviously neither of those things. There's a very
clever, very sharp little brain operating inside that incredibly pretty head of yours. Only someone with a lot
of intelligence and a fast, alert mind could survive with
your sort of handicap. You must spend half your life
avoiding situations that everyone else takes for granted.
And it must be even harder, since you won't admit to
anyone just what that handicap is.' His gaze held hers
relentlessly, and refused to let her look away. 'I am right
about that, aren't I?' he questioned steadily. 'You never
confide in anyone, you just keep fighting it on your own,
struggling through each day, praying that you're not
going to get yourself into a situation you can't handle.
Only, today it happened. You let me force you into it
because you were too damned proud—or too damned
obstinate!—to tell me the truth.'

Charlie was shaking inside, now. No one had ever
talked to her like this, probing deep into something that
she had fought like hell to keep private.

'Want to tell me about that handicap?' Jay invited.
His voice had dropped a tone lower; it was velvet soft
and so inviting that, to her horror, she felt an awful impulse to blurt out absolutely everything.

'Why don't *you* tell *me*?' she threw back at him, furious at her own moment of sudden weakness. 'After all,
you obviously think you know all about it.'

Jay shook his head. 'I don't suppose there's a living
soul in this world that knows all about it—except for
you,' he added, his face quite expressionless now, as if
he were keeping all his own feelings and responses under
very strict control. 'If you'd confided in someone—
someone professionally qualified, or perhaps even a
friend—you might not be in the mess you're in now.
You're going to have to do it sooner or later. You can't
live with a condition like yours indefinitely, it'll cripple
you in the end. That bright, shiny façade which you show

to the world will gradually fade away, you can't keep up a pretence like that for ever. The strain must be killing.'

'I lead a perfectly happy, fulfilling life,' Charlie retorted defiantly. 'I've got friends, a good job, and I get on well with people. I'm not cracking up under any strain, and I'm definitely not the depressed, maladjusted person you're trying to make me out to be!'

He shrugged a little angrily. 'Have it your own way. Don't pretend you're leading a normal life, though,' he warned. 'Do you think it's normal, not being able to stand anyone laying a single finger on you?'

Charlie went ashen. He had said it, he had actually put the whole ugly truth into words! She was vibrating with indignation and shame now; she couldn't look at him, she didn't ever want to meet that shrewd, all-seeing gaze of his again. He had gone straight to the heart of her problem. He hadn't skirted round it, or taken refuge in comforting euphemisms, but had simply stated the blunt truth—that she couldn't bear to be touched.

And how she hated him for knowing that humiliating and highly personal fact about her! Forgetting everything except the inner rage that was swirling through her, whipping up a storm of fierce resentment, she jumped to her feet and confronted him.

'Satisfied?' she demanded in a furious voice. 'I thought anthropology was meant to be your subject. I didn't know you had ambitions to be a psychologist as well, poking around inside my head, trying to find out things that are none of your damned business!'

But Jay didn't even answer her. Instead, his eyes had taken on an expression that she had never seen before, and he definitely wasn't relaxed and laid-back now. He had gone so tense that she could see the outline of his rigid muscles under his supple skin.

Then she realised that, for the first time in three years, she had been stupidly careless. When she had first undressed, she had been careful to keep her back to him, and after that she had remained lying on her stomach. That swift burst of anger and humiliation had sent years of carefully learned caution flying straight out of the window, though. Still wearing only her brief cotton bra and pants, she had jumped up and faced him, forgetting that she was giving him a clear view of something that no one else, except a doctor, had ever seen.

She began to feel totally sick, as Jay's gaze fixed on the flat expanse of skin just above the swell of her breasts. He couldn't seem to look away and, hard though she tried, she just couldn't move, couldn't break away from that disbelieving, riveting stare.

'My God!' he said at last in a taut voice. 'Someone's carved their initials on your skin!'

CHAPTER FOUR

CHARLIE pounded angrily away at the typewriter. She was fully dressed again now, and several hours had passed since Jay had made that last remark, but it was still echoing round and round inside her head. She couldn't forget it; for once she couldn't block it out of her mind.

And the psychologists insisted that it was beneficial to get everything out into the open! she told herself viciously as her fingers hit the keys in a hard, staccato rhythm. What did they know about it? The only way you could get on with your life was never to think about the past; to shut it away behind a tightly locked door and make sure no one ever found the key.

Try opening that door just a fraction and all the horrific memories would start to force their way out; there would be no stopping them.

At least Jay had had the sense not to ask any more questions, and she had been grateful for that. She had simply grabbed her clothes and rushed inside the hut. When she had found the nerve to come out again, a couple of hours later, he had still said very little. The brief snatches of conversation they had exchanged since then had been strictly impersonal, and she had very slowly begun to relax as she had realised he wasn't going to demand an explanation. Yet there wasn't the same relaxed atmosphere that there had been before, and it was never going to be the same again. He *knew*. That single fact was enough to put a mile-high barrier between them, at least as far as she was concerned.

And the worst part of it was that there was no way out. She was stuck here for at least another couple of weeks, right under Jay's nose, day and night. She also had the disturbing feeling that, despite his tactful silence since he had first seen those scars, he wasn't going to let it go at that. Sooner or later, he was going to start asking all sorts of questions, and just the thought of it made her shudder. Why couldn't he understand that she had only survived by burying all the old memories so deep that she could go for days, even weeks now, without thinking about them?

She didn't sleep well that night. After a while, she realised that she was afraid to sleep in case she began to dream. She knew all there was to know about bad dreams; she had had some real humdingers, waking up sweat-soaked and wild-eyed. Tonight, though, to her great relief, the dreams stayed away, and she finally slipped into a restless doze.

In the morning, she crawled out of her hammock to find Jay was already up and cooking breakfast.

'I thought we'd take a break from work this morning,' he said easily. 'We've both worked hard for the last few days. It will do us good to have a couple of hours off, to relax and unwind a little.'

'Doing what?' she asked warily.

'I've been reading through some of Jim's notes. Apparently there's another Indian settlement on the other side of the river. It's a couple of miles into the forest, but according to Jim's records and maps there's a fairly well marked track which shouldn't be too difficult to follow. I thought we could go and take a look at it, see if there's any chance of us making it as far as the settlement.'

Charlie raised her eyebrows. 'And that's your idea of a relaxing break?' she queried caustically. 'A trek through the rain forest, in search of a tribe of Indians?

Did anyone ever tell you that you've got a very weird outlook on life?'

One blue and one green eye fixed on her unblinkingly. 'I see the bright and bouncing Charlotte's back this morning,' he remarked. 'But I don't mind you being rude to me if it means you're feeling better.' And, before she had a chance to comment hotly on that, he went on, 'Can you swim?'

'Swim?' she repeated. 'Of course I can. Why?'

He shot her a dry glance. 'Can you think of any other way of getting across the river?'

'Well—no,' she admitted, slightly deflated. 'Not unless your friend Jim knocked a boat together in his spare time and left it conveniently lying around. Although, considering the state in which he left everything else, it would probably sink the moment we got into it,' she added with a distinct touch of sarcasm.

Jay shot her a warning glance. 'It wasn't Jim's fault that the radio's dead. It was in good working order when he left here.'

Charlie looked unconvinced, but bit back any more sarcastic remarks. She and Jay were going to have to live together for the next couple of weeks, so there was no point in deliberately provoking him. And everyone knew that the one sure way to irritate a man was to criticise his friends—even if that criticism was perfectly justified!

'Are you a good swimmer?' he asked, looking at her closely. 'The river's quite wide, and the current can apparently be fairly strong in the middle. There's no way I'm going to risk taking you across if you can't manage more than a doggy-paddle.'

'Don't worry, I'm not going to sink like a stone after just a few strokes,' she told him a little huffily. 'I might not be able to manage the Channel, but I can certainly get across that river.'

'There's a thick length of heavy cable that stretches from one bank to the other,' Jay told her. 'Like the landing-strip, it was left behind by the oil company after it pulled out. If you find yourself getting into trouble, you can always grab hold of the cable and haul yourself across.'

'What should I wear?'

His gaze flicked over the cotton shorts and T-shirt she had put on that morning. 'They'll do fine. But make sure you're wearing strong-soled sandals, so your feet won't get damaged if you tread on anything sharp.'

An hour later, they made their way down to the river. Where the cable stretched across, rough steps had been cut into the muddy bank, making it easier to get down to the water's edge. Charlie stared across, then bit her lip a little apprehensively. This close, the river looked much wider than it had from a distance. Despite what she had said to Jay earlier, she wasn't a particularly strong swimmer, although she could splash her way up and down a swimming pool without too much trouble. This wasn't a calm, currentless pool, though; the mud-coloured water swirled by slowly but powerfully, deep and somehow mysterious, almost like a living thing.

Rather belatedly, it occurred to her that she didn't *have* to go with Jay. Come to think of it, she should have jumped at the chance of a few quiet hours on her own. So why hadn't she? A little wryly, she admitted to herself that she didn't actually like being on her own in this exotic but isolated place; that she felt a lot better when another human being was around, even if it was only Jay Challoner.

'Ready?' asked Jay, breaking into her thoughts.

'Er—yes,' she answered, slightly nervously.

'You'd better go first, then I'll be right behind you if you get into trouble.'

'I won't,' she assured him, sounding a lot more confident than she felt. She cautiously made her way down the uneven steps, then stepped into the water.

She was soon in deep enough to begin swimming, and it was comforting to know the thick cable was only a couple of yards away, ready to grab hold of if anything went wrong. She was sure it wouldn't, though. She was swimming fairly easily, and when she looked ahead of her, she could see that she was already nearly half-way across.

Giving a grin of satisfaction, she confidently surged forward. Just seconds later, though, the water suddenly felt as if it were physically tugging at her body. Her legs seemed to be pulled to one side, the rest of her went the other way and, before she even had time to gasp with surprise, she found herself being whisked downriver.

Instinct made her grab at the cable as she bobbed past it, and with more luck than judgement she managed to get one hand curled round it. Her arm felt as if it were being wrenched out of its socket, but she sucked in a deep breath and somehow caught hold of the cable with her other hand; then she just hung there, gasping for air.

Gradually, she became aware that Jay was holding on to the cable just behind her.

'I think we just hit the current in the middle of the river,' he told her wryly.

'I think you're probably right,' she agreed breathlessly. 'So, what do we do now?'

'We'd better go back. The current's a lot faster than I thought it would be, it's far too risky to keep going. There might be an even stronger undertow ahead of us.'

That was fine by Charlie; she was getting distinctly fed up with this little adventure. She had been born and raised in a city; this outdoor life was fine in small doses, but she definitely wasn't cut out to be an intrepid explorer.

There was just one small problem. *How* was she going to get back? Right now, she couldn't seem to move one way or the other. She didn't have enough strength in her arms to haul herself along the cable, not with that current trying its hardest to drag her in the opposite direction. And on top of that, her muscles were already beginning to ache painfully, while her fingers were stiff and cramped from gripping the thick wire.

Jay moved a little closer. 'The best solution would be for you to hold on round my waist, then I'll pull us both out of this current. Once we're free of the undertow, we should be able to swim back to the bank without any problems.'

But Charlie didn't like that particular solution at all. 'I can manage,' she told him stiffly. 'Just let me get out of this in my own way.'

'The moment you let go of the cable, you're going to be swept off downriver,' he shot back irritably. 'So what are you planning to do—hang there indefinitely?'

'I'll be all right,' she insisted stubbornly.

His face instantly darkened, and she nervously realised that he was as near as she had ever seen him come to losing his temper completely.

'You will *not* be all right!' he roared at her, his voice booming out over the sound of the swirling water. 'What the hell's wrong with you, Charlotte? Would you rather drown than have to touch me?'

Put like that, she had to concede that he did have a point. She really was behaving rather stupidly. Anyway, despite her defiant words, she had to admit that she really didn't have a lot of choice. The only way she was going to get back to the bank was by clinging on to this man's powerful body.

All the same, she didn't want to do it. Only sheer necessity was forcing her into it. She gave a small inward shudder, then tensely turned to face him. 'What do you want me to do?' she muttered through clenched teeth.

Jay manoeuvred himself along the cable until he was right alongside her. Her body was brushing against his now, as the water tossed them around, and she felt her limbs go rigid. It was either this, or possibly drown, she reminded herself grimly. Of the two ordeals, she supposed this was marginally preferable.

Reaching up, Jay clasped one of her wrists firmly. 'Let go of the cable with this hand,' he instructed.

Trying to ignore the strong fingers which were biting into her skin, she did as he had ordered. A moment later, she felt him guide her free hand to his waist. It seemed odd to be holding on to smooth human skin instead of that rough cable. His body felt warm against her palm, despite the coolness of the water. Then he grasped her other arm and wrapped it round him, so she was tightly grabbing hold of him, and she felt his strong muscles begin to flex and move as he slowly but easily pulled the two of them along the cable.

It didn't take them long to reach the calmer water. As soon as the current stopped tugging at her body, Charlie let go of Jay and struck out on her own.

'I'll be fine now,' she gasped out hurriedly. 'I can get back to the bank without any problems.'

She was rather annoyed to find him swimming right alongside her, as if he wasn't entirely convinced she could get back under her own steam. It seemed to take ages to reach the bank, but at last she was finally scrambling out of the water. She hauled herself exhaustedly up the uneven steps, then she flopped down on the ground and let out a huge sigh of relief at being back on terra firma again. Her legs still felt distinctly wobbly, though, and her heart was pounding a lot harder than usual.

As Jay walked over to join her, she glared up at him.

'Not one of your better ideas,' she remarked with some sarcasm. 'Next time you come up with a bright suggestion for a few hours of fun and relaxation, remind me to ignore you!'

'My only mistake was in taking you along,' Jay answered calmly. 'I should have realised the current would be too strong for a woman to cope with. According to Jim's notes, he's crossed the river several times without any problems, but of course he's always gone on his own.' And before she could make any caustic remarks about the absent Jim, he added, 'Incidentally, it's not a very good idea to flop down like that without first having a very good look around. You could have sat right on top of a poisonous snake.'

'You've already half drowned me—are you trying to scare me to death now?' she demanded.

'Another thing,' he went on, completely ignoring her response. 'You lied to me. You're not a good swimmer, you're hardly even mediocre. Don't you know that lies like that can be dangerous out here?'

But Charlie had had just about enough by now. The entire morning had been a total disaster, and the whole thing had been completely his fault. He was the one who had suggested that crazy river-crossing—since he was supposed to be an expert on this sort of environment, he should have *known* they would end up in trouble.

'I must have been out of my mind to have ever agreed to come here with you in the first place!' she flung at him furiously. 'It was an insane idea, right from the start. No one flies a secretary all the way out from England just so they can sit in the middle of the jungle and write a book.'

'I do,' replied Jay, quite unperturbed.

'Then you're the one who's mad. All that expense—you could have found yourself a secretary right here, in Ecuador, and saved yourself a lot of money.'

'Money's no problem,' Jay replied lazily.

'Well, how very nice for you!' she retorted with a fresh burst of acerbity. 'I suppose you've made so much money from your books that you've run out of things to fritter it away on.'

'The income from those books has certainly added considerably to my bank balance,' he agreed. 'But it was already extremely healthy before I wrote a single word. A few years back, an uncle of mine died, and left me a small fortune.'

Charlie stared at him. 'You're independently wealthy?'

'I'm afraid so. And that means I can well afford to be unconventional now and then, if I feel like it.'

'That's even worse,' she said in disgust. 'It means you're nothing more than a—a playboy!' she finished accusingly.

To her surprise, Jay didn't lose his temper. He didn't even look annoyed. In fact, a moment later, a broad grin crossed his face.

'You've certainly got a lot of old-fashioned ideas stuffed away inside that gorgeous head of yours. What did you *expect* me to do with my money? Give it away? Let it sit in a bank, gathering dust? Neither of those options appealed to me very much, so in the end I decided simply to use it. Not squander it,' he added emphatically. 'I don't think my uncle left me that inheritance so I could fritter it away. But I don't see anything wrong in using it to make life easier—especially where work's concerned.'

'It was still a waste of money, bringing me all the way out here,' she insisted stubbornly.

Jay lightly lifted one eyebrow. 'I thought it was a very practical arrangement. I couldn't be certain of finding a decent secretary once I arrived in Ecuador. And, although you're a bit of a pain at times, you're definitely very competent. More than that, though, I got the feeling right from the start that we would work well together. That was more important to me than any financial consideration. It's an asset that money literally can't buy.'

'And your one big mistake,' Charlie muttered.

His gaze narrowed slightly. 'Do you think so? We were getting along well enough until I saw those scars.' Ignoring the sudden tension that visibly shot through her, he went on. 'And the only reason you're so edgy and bad-tempered right now is because you had to hold on to me in that river. You hated having to physically touch me. You'd rather die than admit it, but you're still shaking inside. I'm right, Charlotte, aren't I?' he went on with relentless persistence.

She raised her head and glared at him fiercely. 'Why do you keep calling me that? Since you seem to know just about everything else about me, you must know that I hate it!'

'Because someone else used to call you by your full name?' Jay guessed perceptively. 'Someone you don't want to remember?' He paused, then added softly, 'Want to tell me about it?'

'No, I don't,' she shot back instantly. 'It's none of your damned business!'

He studied her reflectively. 'I could make it my business,' he said at last.

'What do you mean by that?' she demanded very warily.

Jay stretched himself out beside her, and she had the sudden, vivid impression that this casual approach was quite deliberate, that he was forcing himself to remain relaxed so that he wouldn't scare her off. He was treating her like a nervous pet, she told herself with a rush of pure indignation. One that he had only just acquired and which deeply interested him, making him determined to find out more about its background and habits. Well, he could just forget about that little idea! She wasn't here just to provide him with an entertaining diversion whenever he began to feel bored.

His eyes were fixed on her again now, and Charlie very much wished that they weren't. She kept getting the feeling that they had the ability to see far too much. Why wouldn't he just get up, walk away and leave her alone? She supposed that she could always jump to her feet and stalk off if this interrogation got too much to handle, but she had already admitted to herself that she didn't want to do that. It would have been too much like an admission of defeat; he would know that he had really started to get to her.

'Do you want to know what I think?' Jay mused, a few moments later.

'No,' she denied emphatically. 'I'm not in the least interested.'

'I'll tell you anyway,' Jay went on comfortably. 'I think that you hate the full version of your name because someone taught you to hate it. And the same person taught you to hate being touched. You soon learned it had pretty unpleasant consequences. But, whoever that bastard was, he's not around any longer, Charlotte. So perhaps it's time you began to learn some new lessons.'

Despite her determination not to get involved in this, she somehow couldn't stop herself asking, 'What sort of lessons?'

A brief flicker of satisfaction showed on Jay's face, as if he was pleased by her answer.

'Quite simple ones. For a start, I could keep using your full name—Charlotte—until you finally stop flinching every time you hear it.'

She bit her lip. 'Do I really flinch?' she asked reluctantly at last.

'Yes, you do. Don't worry,' he added, seeing the unhappy look on her face, 'I shouldn't think anyone else ever notices the way you react. It's no more than a slight twitch of your muscles.'

'*You* noticed,' she pointed out tensely.

'I'm more observant than most people,' came his calm response.

Charlie wondered why she didn't find his reply particularly comforting.

'The second lesson's going to be a lot harder, though,' Jay went on. 'Someone's got to try and teach you how to enjoy physical contact with other human beings again.'

'And are you volunteering for that impossible task?' she enquired with deliberate sarcasm.

'If you like.'

That did it. Her nerves would only ever stand a certain amount of strain, and he had definitely just nudged them over the limit. Her eyes suddenly blazed as she swung round to confront him.

'I definitely *don't* like!'

Jay still refused to lose his own temper. 'How can you be so sure, unless you at least give it a try?'

'How can I be sure?' she echoed with some vehemence. 'I'll tell you. If a certain food makes you ill, you don't eat it. If you get seasick, then you stay well away from boats.'

One dark eyebrow lifted questioningly. 'So, if physical contact makes you want to scream out loud with revulsion, you avoid the entire human race? Not a very practical solution, Charlotte.'

'I don't avoid—everyone,' she got out through gritted teeth.

His eyes flickered alertly. 'No? Who can you stand to touch, then? Other women, perhaps? Children? Older men, who don't seem any threat? But you didn't like touching me,' he reminded her softly. 'So it looks as if we've narrowed the field down considerably. It's not just general contact that's the problem. It's *sexual* contact.'

Charlie clapped her hands over her ears. 'Stop it! I don't want to hear any more of this. It feels like you're getting right inside my head, and you've no right to do that, no right at all!'

'Maybe not,' Jay agreed, and his own voice had suddenly taken on an unexpectedly fierce note. 'But inside your head's exactly where I want to be, because that's where all the answers are locked away.' He paused briefly, then went on in a more even tone. 'When I was a kid, I used to get a real kick out of fixing things that were broken. Even now, when I see something that doesn't work, I get this compulsion to tinker around with it, to try and put it right again.'

'If you want to tinker with something, try the radio,' Charlie retorted a little desperately. 'That definitely doesn't work, and you can't do any harm messing around with a few broken wires. But I'm a *person*, Jay. If you start interfering in something you don't understand, you could just make things a lot worse.'

He stared at her a trifle grimly. 'Could they really get any worse? Come on, Charlotte, let's have the truth for once.' And, when she didn't answer, he shook his head. 'All right, I'll drop the subject for now. But I'm going to come back to it later, I promise you that. And, like it or not, you're not going to be able to run away from it. You're stuck here, you can't get away from me. I can back you right into a corner if I want to, and keep you there for as long as I like.' As she stared up at him with huge, horrified eyes, he nodded slowly and inexorably. 'That's right, this is it. Crunch time. By the time you finally get out of here, at least you'll know if this phobia of yours is curable or not. One way or another, we're going to find out over the next few days.'

Charlie spent the rest of the day totally on edge. By comparison, Jay seemed relaxed and even rather pleased with life. He walked around humming tunelessly to himself, and finally took himself off for a couple of hours' fishing, leaving Charlotte to get on with a pile of typing. He behaved as if nothing out of the ordinary had happened this morning, and didn't once refer to the tense conversation they had had.

This was all getting to be completely bizarre, Charlie told herself as she pounded away at the typewriter. After all, he couldn't force her into some sort of amateur psychotherapy session. In fact, he couldn't force her to do anything at all, not if she decided she didn't want to and totally refused to co-operate.

But that was where the rather disturbing bit came into it, because somewhere inside her head a traitorous little voice kept whispering that perhaps this wasn't such a bad idea, that it was time she made some sort of effort to get herself sorted out.

I don't need sorting out! she argued fiercely with herself, ripping a sheet of paper out of the machine and winding in a fresh one. I'm coping fine the way I am, and Jay Challoner had better keep his interfering nose out of my affairs, or I'm going to get really mad!

Later on, she had to endure another restless, sleepless night. It was all the more galling because she had to lie there and listen to Jay's quiet, even breathing as he slept deeply and peacefully, relaxed as a cat, while her own nerves were totally frazzled. In the morning, she was still completely strung-up, waiting all the time for Jay to do or say something that would set all her inner alarm bells ringing. He spent half the morning dictating, though, his voice crisp and unemotional, his mind obviously concentrating solely on the progress of his novel. Charlie finally began to wonder, with a small burst of optimism, if he had just been joking yesterday, winding her up for some obscure reason of his own. She had to admit that it didn't seem very likely, but it was a small ray of hope to cling on to.

Early in the afternoon, the sun blazed down so fiercely that work was quite impossible. The inside of the hut was absolutely stifling, so Jay spread a blanket out in the shade of a nearby tree; then he gestured to Charlie to come and join him.

'When it gets this hot, you just have to sit it out until it cools off again,' he told her, sprawling out lethargically.

Charlie looked down at him nervously. She would have much preferred to have gone and sat by herself under one of the other trees, but she suspected it would be useless to try such a thing. If she grabbed a blanket and went off, he would just get up and follow her. There was absolutely no escape from the damned man!

Her skin prickling uncomfortably, she rather primly sat down on the very edge of the blanket. After a while, though, as Jay sat with his eyes shut, not moving a muscle, she began to unwind just a fraction. It was too hot to get worked up over anything. The heat seemed to be blasting down on them, even the dark patches of shade beneath the tree didn't seem to give much relief from it. No matter how hot it got, though, the high humidity never let up. The forest seemed to be gently steaming as the heavy shower that had drenched it this morning began to evaporate. Charlie's cotton shirt and shorts were sticking to her body, her hair clung damply to her head, and her skin glistened with a light film of moisture.

Jay gave a small grunt and rolled over, making her jump slightly, instantly on her guard again.

'Why don't you lie down?' he suggested lazily. 'It's too hot to do anything except sleep.'

'I'm all right,' she told him stiffly. 'I—I like sitting up.'

He opened one eye—the blue one—and studied her thoughtfully. 'I won't jump on you, if that's what you're scared of,' he said finally. 'I promise you that.'

Charlie sniffed. 'Yesterday, you promised something very different. You said——' She stopped abruptly. She didn't want to remind him of what he had said, just in case he took it into his head to do something about it right this very moment.

He merely smiled, though. 'I know exactly what I said,' he assured her, causing her several moments of complete consternation. 'But I'm still trying to figure out the right way of going about it. For now, let's just forget about it and relax.'

How could she relax? Charlie asked herself in silent indignation. All the same, she finally had to admit that, in this heat, it required too much effort to do anything else. Cautiously, she eased herself down on to the blanket, then made herself comfortable.

For a while, she gazed up at the tiny patches of blue sky that she could see through the thick canopy of leaves overhead, letting vivid flashes of sunlight filter through to the ground below. It seemed unnaturally quiet this afternoon, as if even the birds and the howler monkeys had taken themselves off for a quiet siesta, until it got cooler. Only the faint drone of insects interrupted the silence, like a rather hypnotic background hum.

Charlie felt herself slowly relaxing, her eyes were starting to get very heavy now. In just a moment, she knew they were going to close and she would doze off. Then she caught the faintest flicker of movement to her left. She instantly turned her head, only to find that Jay had opened his own eyes now, and his gaze was fixed on her in a way that immediately sent a jolt of alarm straight through her.

Suddenly wide awake again, she was just about to spring up nervously, when he lazily lifted one hand.

'It's all right, stay where you are. I'm only looking.'

'Why?' she demanded suspiciously.

'Because I like beautiful things. And you are beautiful, Charlotte.'

Her nerves gave their usual twitch at the sound of her name; yet somehow it wasn't so strong this time, and she had the uncomfortable feeling that he knew it. Certainly, his mouth had relaxed into a rather satisfied smile.

His gaze finally moved on, drifting slowly downwards. A little too late, she realised that her clothes were sticking to her damp skin so closely that they must have left little to the imagination. Instantly embarrassed, she glanced down at herself and saw her body as Jay was seeing it: slim and supple, her skin glowing, as if lightly oiled, her breasts—even her nipples—clearly outlined against the damp cotton, her hips and thighs flowing in complementary curves and lines.

'I'm only looking,' Jay reminded her quietly. 'Not touching.'

'I still don't like it,' came her edgy retort.

'But you haven't run away,' he pointed out with some satisfaction. 'Do you think we're beginning to make some progress?'

She didn't want to talk about it, so she determinedly closed her eyes and hoped he would take the hint.

'Don't shut me out,' Jay ordered firmly. His voice suddenly sounded very much nearer, and her eyes shot open again in alarm. Then she gulped hard. He had raised himself up on one elbow now, and was lying right beside her, looking down at her. Parts of his body were no more than inches away, although there was no actual physical contact between them. He didn't come any closer, though, and he kept quite still, as if determined not to alarm her further.

'Our bodies can behave very strangely at times,' he remarked at last, in a calm yet thoughtful tone. 'They can go on being afraid of things long after there's any need to be. Sometimes you just have to grit your teeth and teach them how to behave normally again, stick at it until they finally understand that there's nothing to be scared of any longer.'

'I don't want those sort of lessons!' Charlie retorted sharply.

'Then how about a small experiment?' he suggested, and she had the awful feeling that he wasn't going to give up on this until he had had his way. He held up his hand. 'You see this?'

'Of course.' She gazed at it for an instant, uneasily noting the strength in his fingers and wrists. She knew that this man was so much more physically powerful than she was, that he could force her to do just about anything he wanted, if he set his mind to it.

'It's just a hand,' Jay went on, his voice low now, and totally relaxed. The dark velvet tones washed over her with a curious, almost hypnotic effect, somehow draining a fraction of the tension from her stiff body. 'It can't harm you, it's just skin and flesh, muscle and bone. So— there's no need to panic when I let it rest against your stomach—like this——'

And somehow—she still wasn't sure how it had happened—his hand was lying lightly on the flat area between her hips, warm and steady. She could feel the outline of his fingers and palm imprinted there, and she stared up at him in disbelief.

'You said you wouldn't touch me!' she cried. 'Get off. Get *off*!'

She wanted to wriggle frantically away, but she just couldn't move. It was always like this, she just seemed to freeze up completely when someone touched her, as if her entire body had become paralysed.

'What do you feel?' asked Jay immediately, his face and tone suddenly vividly alert again now. 'I want to know *exactly*.'

'Sick!' she spat at him.

'Physically sick? You actually want to throw up?'

His unexpected questions forced her to think about it. For a moment, she even forgot about his hand scorching its heat against her shrinking skin.

'No,' she admitted reluctantly at last. 'Just sort of— nauseous, as if I've just got off a roundabout and my stomach hasn't settled down yet.'

'That's tension,' he told her. 'Your muscles are so rigid, it's affecting your digestive system. Take a few slow, deep breaths. Let the tension just dissolve away, until your body gradually goes limp.'

'It won't work,' she muttered, but somehow she found herself doing what he had suggested. And it was funny, but her muscles did seem to be relaxing a little. She could almost feel the tension gradually trickling away.

'How do you feel now?' Jay asked, a few minutes later.

'A bit better,' she rather grudgingly admitted. 'But I still don't like you touching me,' she warned.

'But you don't actually hate it any more?'

'Well—no——'

'And you don't feel sick?'

'I suppose not.'

'Good,' said Jay, with some satisfaction. 'So let's move on to lesson two.'

'What's that?' demanded Charlie suspiciously.

'Learning that having someone touching you can be nice. Very, *very* nice.'

Panic instantly fluttered through her again. She wasn't ready for this, she hadn't even got used yet to the light touch of his hand on her stomach. All right, so she didn't feel sick any more; she wasn't even shaking, which was quite remarkable, now that she came to think about it. Even so——

'Just lie still, keep breathing slowly and evenly, and let yourself drift,' Jay instructed in that quiet, relaxed voice that was so astonishingly easy to obey.

'I want this to stop right now,' Charlie somehow got out, but even she could hear the lack of conviction in her voice.

Jay looked down at her consideringly. 'No, I don't think you want me to stop,' he said at last. 'I think you're as curious as I am to know what's going to happen when I move my hand like this—and like this——'

His fingers seemed to be drifting at random, floating a few inches one way, briefly pausing, then sliding softly over to another part of her stomach. Charlie found herself filled with total amazement. She had never realised a man's touch could be so incredibly gentle.

'Not too bad?' queried Jay, with a pleased smile. 'OK, then let's try something else.'

Before she had a chance to protest, he shifted position slightly, and she felt that inner trembling start up again as his dark bulk loomed over her, reminding her of his size, his powerfulness. He still wasn't touching her with any part of his body except his hand, though, so she didn't feel too badly threatened. After a while, the trembling eased off a little, allowing her to relax slightly again.

'Just remember,' Jay told her, 'I'll never force you to do anything you don't want to do.'

Her eyes opened very wide and she stared up at him with a fresh surge of indignation.

'How on earth can you say that? I never wanted to get involved with this stupid experiment in the first place!'

'Yes, you did,' he replied calmly. 'If you'd really been totally against it, I'd never have laid a finger on you.'

'How clever of you to know exactly what I'm thinking and feeling, what I want and don't want,' she flung back at him. 'How do you manage that little trick?'

Jay refused to let her goad him. 'No trick,' came his easy response. 'Just more experience than you'd probably approve of. And perhaps something else,' he added thoughtfully, after a moment's hesitation. 'Like it or not, Charlotte, we seem to operate on the same wavelength. It's something that happens between two people sometimes. I sensed it the moment I first saw you, that's why I knew we'd work well together. And, if we're mentally compatible, there's no reason why we shouldn't be physically compatible as well.'

'You've got it all worked out, haven't you?' Charlie muttered, with a touch of resentment. 'I suppose it's going to be your way of amusing yourself over the next couple of weeks. Get little Charlotte straightened out, and send her back to civilisation as a fit member of society. You'd get a real kick out of that, wouldn't you? What everyone likes to call "job satisfaction".'

Jay's eyes flickered warningly. 'That's not why I'm doing this.'

'Then why are you going to all this trouble?' she challenged. 'Because you feel *sorry* for me? That's even worse,' she rushed on. 'Having someone going around pitying you—it makes you feel about two inches tall!'

Jay's patience finally evaporated, and sheer irritation blazed out of his face as he abruptly swung himself closer.

'You want to know why I'm doing this?' he growled. 'It's because you're young and you're gorgeous, and it's criminal that you shouldn't get a little pleasure out of a simple thing like this——'

Before she could stop him or yell out a vehement protest, he had lowered his head, letting his mouth close over hers with firm determination.

For just a split second, Charlie found herself unexpectedly fascinated by the sensation of his lips brushing against hers. She was vividly aware of a sense of warmth, even of shared excitement. Then the pressure increased, the excitement abruptly vanished, and the old sense of being trapped began to surge over her. An instant later, she was grimly fighting him, kicking out indiscriminately, not caring how much damage she was inflicting.

Jay let go of her immediately. His breathing was a little faster, there was a faint flare of colour to his face, and she was briefly swept by the impression that bringing that kiss to such an abrupt halt was one of the hardest things he had ever done.

She didn't care, though. She was free, and that was the only important thing. Rolling clear of him, she jumped to her feet; then glared down at him.

'I told you this wouldn't work. You had no right even to try it. Just stay away from me in future!'

But as she swiftly walked away from him, not allowing herself to look back, there was an odd ache deep in the pit of her stomach. And, after a while, to her total astonishment, she realised that it was caused by a sharp surge of savage disappointment.

CHAPTER FIVE

JAY left Charlie on her own for over an hour before finally strolling over to rejoin her. As his shadow fell over her, she looked up and scowled.

'Go away. I don't want to talk to you.'

'That's childish,' he pointed out reasonably.

'I know,' mumbled Charlie, hating herself for behaving like this, but still so shaken up inside that she couldn't seem to stop.

Jay frowned. 'I only wanted to apologise. I took the whole thing far too fast. I don't know what the hell came over me. Don't worry, it won't happen again.'

'Too damned right, it won't!' she retorted. 'I'm fed up to the back teeth with you meddling with what's going on inside my head. Try it again and I'll—I'll——'

Since she couldn't think of any threat that would be in the least effective against him, she lapsed into a rather sulky silence.

Unexpectedly, Jay laughed. 'Do you think I'm going to give up on this? I'm not. What's more, if you were really honest with yourself, I think you'd admit you don't want me to. You're already half-way there, Charlotte,' he went on encouragingly. 'You're getting to the stage where you *want* to break out of this cage that you've locked yourself into. So why not go for it, take a chance? See if, between us, we can't find a way of smashing down those bars?'

But she had fought this for so long on her own that she just wasn't ready to accept help from the first man who rolled up and offered it.

'Impressive speech,' she scoffed, 'but I was about to suggest something very different. You brought me out here to work, so let's get on with *that*. No more digging around in each other's personal lives, and definitely no more amateur psychology. From now on, I want to get back to a proper boss/secretary relationship. I'm certain things will run more smoothly if we both try and stick to our respective roles.'

'Keeping everything very formal?'

'That's it exactly,' she agreed at once, pleased that he had cottoned on so quickly. 'I'm sure it'll work out much better for both of us that way.'

'Perhaps you're right,' Jay agreed, his tone so affable that she was instantly suspicious. 'So—let's see if I've got this straight. We'll sit in our hut in the middle of the rain forest, we'll work from nine to five with just a short lunch-break, and then we'll retire to our hammocks for the night?'

Charlie scowled irritably. 'There's no need for sarcasm! I know it won't be like a proper office atmosphere, but I still think we can make it work, if we try.'

'And does this new arrangement mean that I can chase you round the desk, when I'm in the mood?' enquired Jay with some interest. 'That's the boss's privilege, if I remember rightly.'

At that, she lost the battle to hold on to her temper. 'Will you stop winding me up?' she yelled.

'Probably not,' he said cheerfully. 'I think it's good for you to show some honest, genuine emotion every now and then.' Then he added slyly, 'Incidentally, that's really no way to talk to your boss. Carry on like that, and you could get fired.'

'The sooner the better!' she flung at his departing back, as he casually ambled off, picking up his fishing-rod and then heading towards the river.

Once he was out of sight, Charlie subsided into a bad-tempered heap, and glared furiously at the trees all around her. What wouldn't she give to get out of here? This place was really starting to get on her nerves, and they had barely been here a week yet. What kind of state was she going to be in when the pilot finally picked them up? She would probably be completely raving, she told herself gloomily. And it would all be Jay Challoner's fault. Touching her, kissing her, when he knew she couldn't stand it. Quite deliberately, she had wiped from her mind the memory of how he had coaxed her into accepting the touch of his hand.

Yet for the next couple of days, much to her surprise, Jay seemed to be going along with her suggestion that they should get things back on to a more formal footing between them. At least, as formal as they could be, considering they were both living in a small hut and sleeping just a few feet away from each other at night. He kept all conversation on a strictly impersonal level, made no more attempts to touch her, and generally kept a reasonable distance between them.

Charlie eventually began to breathe a little more easily. It was a great relief that everything was going so unexpectedly smoothly. And, on top of that, the book was fairly racing along. She often had to work flat out to keep up with Jay's output. She didn't mind that, though, she had always been good at hard work. Anyway, it kept her mind off other, rather more disturbing thoughts.

They took it in turns to cope with the meals. Since Charlie usually cooked breakfast, she rolled out of her hammock early one morning at the end of the week, had a quick wash-down with a bucket of river-water, then sleepily pulled on some fresh clothes. Jay was still sprawled out in his hammock—he seemed to have the enviable ability to stretch out and sleep for as long as he chose—so she crept past him, not wanting to wake him. All the same, she couldn't resist a quick peep round the blanket that curtained off his sleeping area. As always, she was left with the impression of a giant cat, peacefully slumbering. One small sound, though, and she knew those bi-coloured eyes would snap open, and Jay would be instantly awake and alert, so she was careful to be as quiet as possible.

She stuck her head out through the doorway to the hut; then she gave a small sigh of satisfaction. On mornings like these, with the sun filtering down from a hazy blue sky, macaws and parrots flapping around overhead, showing off their dazzling colours, and other less exotic but just as fascinating birds singing their heads off in the nearby trees, things never seemed quite so bad. Even the racket set up by the howler monkeys didn't get on her nerves quite as much as usual. Charlie knew there were other animals out there, too, but so far she hadn't actually seen any. Not that she was particularly anxious to come face to face with a jaguar, or a wild pig! It wasn't very likely, though. Jay had told her that, since a lot of the animals were hunted by the Indians for food, they went out of their way to avoid any contact with human beings.

She stretched luxuriously, soaking up the early morning sunshine, making the most of it before it got too hot. Then something tickled her leg. She absently bent down to brush off the small insect that was crawling up her calf, but an instant later she gave a loud yelp of surprise and snatched back her hand.

In a second, Jay was standing beside her, his brows drawn together. 'What's up?'

'Something bit me,' she complained. 'Ow, it *hurts*!'

He caught hold of her hand, then looked at it closely. 'What was it? Did you see it?' he queried sharply.

'It looked like a large ant,' Charlie told him miserably, as the pain got even worse. 'Just a stupid ant. I didn't think the damned thing would turn vicious and bite me. I was only trying to brush it off my leg.'

'I'm sure it was nothing personal,' Jay assured her drily. 'Ants around here are inclined to bite fairly indiscriminately. They haven't decided to wage some kind of vendetta against you.'

But she wasn't in the mood for humour, even if he was only trying to cheer her up—and she wasn't altogether sure that he was. He could just be enjoying her discomfort, she told herself dolefully.

'Can't you do something about it?' she moaned, a fresh burst of misery sweeping over her as her finger throbbed with increasing waves of pain. 'There's got to be something in that medical kit that can cure a silly little thing like an ant bite.'

'There's nothing silly about a bite from one of the ants around here,' he warned. 'Several of them can deliver a sizeable sting. If you've been bitten by a konga ant—and from the way you're acting I'd say that's highly possible—then it's going to hurt like hell for at least a couple of hours.'

'Can't you put some sort of cream on it, to take away some of the pain?' she persisted.

Jay shook his head. 'You'll just have to sit it out, I'm afraid. You're lucky in one way. The bite doesn't have any serious side-effects, it's just incredibly painful.'

'I don't feel very lucky,' she grumbled, nursing her hand.

He shrugged. 'I'll dab some antiseptic cream on it, but apart from that there's not much I can do except offer tea and sympathy. One thing—it'll make you a bit more careful in future, teach you that it's a good idea to treat the insects around here with some respect.'

Charlie glared at him balefully. 'Is that your idea of sympathy?' she got out through gritted teeth.

'I'm afraid so,' came his cheerful response. 'I'll go and make the tea. I'll only be a few minutes.'

But when he came back with a mug of tea, she couldn't drink it. She just sat in a huddle, cradling her hand, her eyes brimming over with tears of utter misery. It felt as if someone was trying to twist her bitten finger right off. The thought of having to put up with the excruciating sensation for a couple of more hours was sending her plummeting into a black depression.

Jay took a tube of antiseptic cream from his pocket, smeared some on her throbbing finger, then settled himself down beside her. 'I suppose this means you won't be able to work this morning,' he remarked after a couple of minutes.

Charlie lifted her head and stared at him incredulously, her tears briefly forgotten. 'I don't believe you just said that! Here I am, practically writhing in agony, and you're complaining because I'm not going to be able to work for a couple of hours?'

'You're the one who laid out all the ground-rules, and who insisted that we stick to a rigid working routine,' he reminded her.

'And I'm not allowed to take any sick-leave?' she retorted with sarcasm.

Jay's gaze fixed on her blandly. 'You're not sick, you've just been bitten by an ant,' came his cool reply.

She shook her head in disbelief. This was incredible—how could he behave like this? Where was the man she had got to know—sometimes, almost to like—over the past few days? The man who had shown unexpected flashes of sympathy, a surprising gentleness, a sense of understanding that she had unconsciously come to rely on more and more?

'What's the matter with you?' she demanded. 'Haven't you got any feelings?'

Jay's expression instantly altered, his eyes becoming several shades more intense.

'Oh, yes, I've got feelings,' he assured her. 'But you've made it perfectly clear that you don't want me to show them. You only feel comfortable if I keep them locked away.'

A glimmer of understanding began to break through, briefly distracting her from the pain in her hand. 'Oh, I think I get it,' she said slowly. 'This is another of your little lessons, isn't it? You want me to admit that I don't like it when you act as if you don't give a damn about me.'

'That's up to you,' Jay answered equably. 'I don't want you to admit any such thing unless that's the way you really feel. Lies aren't any good in this sort of situation, Charlotte.'

She sat and thought about that one for a while. She was still mad at the way he was playing psychological games with her, but at the same time she had to admit he had a point. She hadn't liked it when he hadn't shown a jot of concern.

'I suppose I wouldn't mind a bit of genuine sympathy,' she conceded reluctantly at last.

His mouth relaxed into a faint smile. 'That isn't too hard to supply.' A moment later, he took hold of her hand and folded it inside his own; then he began to soothingly rub her bitten finger.

And it was odd, but it really did seem to take the edge off the pain. Charlie gave a small sigh of relief, and began to feel life wasn't so bad, after all.

'We seem to be making quite a lot of progress,' Jay remarked after a couple of minutes.

She stared up at him with new wariness. 'What do you mean?'

'I'm sitting here, holding your hand, and I haven't heard a single squeak of alarm out of you,' he pointed out. 'A couple of days ago, you'd have had hysterics if I'd tried anything like this.'

She blinked hard. She hadn't even given it a second thought; she had just let him take hold of her hand as if it were the most natural thing in the world. Extraordinary!

'Don't think about it too much,' advised Jay. 'Try and analyse it, and you could end up right back at square one. Just go along with it and let things happen.'

But she didn't quite like the sound of that. Who knew where it could end? And, anyway, what sort of things did he have in mind?

If she could just drag her mind away from that continuous ache in her finger for a couple of minutes, she would ask him. Then again, perhaps she wouldn't, she decided rather hurriedly. It might be better for her peace of mind if she didn't know.

'We're really not doing too badly,' Jay said reflectively, a couple of minutes later. 'We've been here over a week, and this is the first time one of us has been bitten by something.'

'And, of course, it had to be me,' sniffed Charlie, sinking back into a trough of self-pity.

Jay grinned. 'I don't think that someone up there's deliberately picking on you. It's just that I'm more used to this sort of environment, I'm better at spotting things with a painful bite and keeping out of their way.'

'Well, I was born and brought up in a big city. About the only thing likely to bite you was the bad-tempered dog next door,' Charlie muttered. 'All these trees and birds, and back-to-nature stuff—it's all right in small dollops, but it gets a bit much at times.'

'Especially when it turns round and stings you on the hand,' Jay agreed gravely. Then he went on casually, 'Which city were you born in?'

'Manchester,' she answered. Without thinking where this conversation could eventually lead, she added, 'How about you?'

'London.'

'Do your family still live there?'

Jay shook his head. 'We all seem to have inherited more than our fair share of wanderlust. My brother emigrated to Australia several years ago, and my parents are also out there at the moment, on a prolonged visit. And my sister lives in California. When I've finished the American lecture tour, I plan to go and see her, perhaps even stay with her for a while.'

'It must be nice to have brothers and sisters, even if they are scattered round the world,' Charlie said, a little wistfully.

'You haven't got any?'

'No.'

'What about your parents? Are they still living in Manchester?'

Charlie hesitated for a moment, then finally admitted, 'My father walked out on us when I was only a baby. I never knew him. And about three years ago, my mother met a Canadian, a really nice man. Once she thought I was settled, she went back to Canada with him.'

Jay's eyes narrowed perceptively. 'When you were settled—do you mean, when you got married?'

All Charlie's defences instantly slammed into place. How had he got her on to the one subject she didn't want to talk about? She had better watch out, this man was *devious*.

'Why did your uncle leave you all that money?' she asked, deciding it was definitely time to change the subject. 'Why didn't your brother and sister get an equal share?'

'I was the eldest,' explained Jay. 'And my uncle had fairly old-fashioned views about the family loot being handed down from eldest son to eldest son, so I ended up with the lot.'

Charlie frowned. 'That's hardly fair. Didn't your brother and sister resent being left out?'

'Not in the least,' said Jay easily. 'As a matter of fact, I wanted to split it three ways with them, but they wouldn't accept a penny. They were both building new lives for themselves, Alec in Australia and Jenny in California, and they wanted to make it on their own. We're a rather independent lot,' he finished wryly. Then he glanced at her. 'How's your hand now?'

'It feels as if someone's squeezed my finger in a vice,' she grimaced. 'Keep talking, it takes my mind off the pain. Why did you give up anthropology and go off on those crazy trips?'

'I didn't really give it up completely,' Jay answered. 'I just branched out in a rather different direction.'

Charlie gave a loud snort. 'You're not trying to tell me those two books you wrote were based on serious research?'

'They weren't intended as dry and dusty text books,' he agreed. 'But they weren't entirely frivolous.'

'And the fact that they've netted you a small fortune is just coincidental?' she queried with a hint of cynicism.

'I told you, I didn't need the money.'

'Then why did you do it?'

He hesitated, as if he wasn't used to having to explain his motives to anyone. Finally, though, he said, 'I'd led a fairly academic life up until then. The field trips had been interesting, the research was often fascinating, and I'd even been lucky enough to have made a couple of fairly major contributions to my particular field. But I began to feel I was getting into a rut. It wasn't what I wanted to do for the rest of my life. When that inheritance from my uncle suddenly turned up out of the blue, I decided it was time to break out and try something new.'

'So you skipped off to spend a year with the Eskimos,' Charlie commented slightly scathingly. 'Then you dragged some poor girl off to live in the wilds of Africa with you.'

'That "poor girl" did very nicely out of it,' Jay reminded her with some acerbity. 'She gets a percentage of the royalties from the book, and right now she's in Hollywood negotiating a film contract. And she went into the whole thing willingly in the first place. She knew exactly what to expect. I explained everything to her in great detail—including the fact that one of the main themes of the book was going to be the way in which any personal relationship developed between us.'

Which rather shot down Charlie's theory that he had just used the girl, that she really hadn't known what she was letting herself in for.

'Do you still see her?' she asked, and was surprised to find that she had tensed up a little as she waited for his answer.

'No, I don't. One thing we discovered during those months was that we definitely weren't compatible.'

'And your other girlfriend walked out on you after you'd spent that winter with the Eskimos,' she reminded him. 'It looks as if I'm not the only one who has problems getting along with people.'

Jay's eyes flashed a warning at her. 'I've had a couple of relationships that haven't worked out. That doesn't make me some kind of social misfit.'

'You're not married,' she pointed out. 'Most men are, by the time they've reached your age.'

'I suppose I've just never met anyone who's got all the qualities it would need to get me hooked on a long-term relationship. I don't even know what those qualities are, only that I've not come across them so far. And if you think I'm not making much sense, try and look at it from your own point of view. What attracted you to the man you married? What qualities did *he* have that you didn't see in anyone else?'

Charlie felt herself go physically cold. 'That's my business,' she mumbled. 'I don't have to talk about it with you.'

Jay looked at her with a light frown of concern. 'Your hand's suddenly gone like ice. Do you feel ill? That insect bite's not supposed to have any side-effects, but you might be getting some sort of allergic reaction.'

She nearly laughed out loud, but stopped herself just in time, terrified that it might come out as a hysterical cackle.

'I'm fine,' she somehow got out at last.

His frown deepened. 'Then what caused that sudden chill?' His face abruptly changed and hardened. 'It was just after I mentioned your husband. Those scars—by God, was he the man——?'

'I've told you a dozen times, I don't want to talk about it,' Charlie cut in, fighting hard to keep her teeth from audibly chattering. 'It's—it's personal, private. If I was going to tell anyone about it, it would be someone I knew really well, not some—some stranger.'

Jay's brows drew together darkly. 'If you think of me as a stranger, how come you're letting me sit this close and hold your hand? How long is it since you've been this near to a man, Charlotte? How many of them have you let lay a single finger on you?'

Totally shaken—because it was the truth—she turned her head and stared at him. 'But I've never told anyone what really happened,' she whispered. 'Why should I tell you?'

'Because if you don't, it's going to stay locked inside you for ever,' Jay answered a little roughly. 'It's already half crippled you. Eventually, it'll shrivel you up completely, because no one can live with something like that. So talk to me, Charlotte. Lead up to it slowly, if you like. Start by telling me how you met your husband—begin with just his name——'

'Philip Ashborne,' Charlie muttered at last, after a long, tense pause. And somehow that seemed the hardest thing she had ever done in her life, getting out just those two words. 'His name was Philip Ashborne.' She stopped abruptly, took a couple of uneven breaths, then began to speak quickly, as if she had to try and get it all out before she realised what she was doing, and just clammed up.

'I was working on a small local paper,' she went on in an unsteady voice. 'It wasn't much of a paper, mostly advertisements, with just a few short articles about things of local interest, but I enjoyed the job. I used to cover local events, interview people who had done something newsworthy, that sort of stuff. Nothing earthshaking, but it was all good experience. Then, one day, the editor called me in and asked if I'd like to tackle a series of features on local houses with an historical background. I thought it was a good idea, so I started to make a list of houses which fell into that category. Then I began doing some background research into each of them, to see if they were interesting enough to fit into the feature.'

'And one of those houses belonged to Philip Ashborne?' guessed Jay, studying her face with that clear perceptiveness which was becoming so familiar to her.

Charlie nodded. 'Ashborne Hall. I was fascinated by it, even before I visited it,' she said in a low voice, speaking more slowly now. 'It had a history stretching right back to the Middle Ages. Members of the Ashborne family had often been prominent at Court; others had been generals, famous lawyers, or had gone into politics. That was all in the past, though. Now, there was

FREE BOOKS CERTIFICATE

Dear Susan,

Your special introductory offer of 4 free books is too good to miss. I understand they are mine to keep with the free clock. Please also reserve a Reader Service subscription for me. If I decide to subscribe, I shall receive four brand new Masquerade romances every other month for just £6.00, post and packing free. If I decide not to subscribe, I shall write to you within 10 days. The free books are mine to keep in any case.

I understand that I may cancel or suspend my subscription at any time by writing to you. I am over 18 years of age.

4A8M

Name _____
(BLOCK CAPITALS PLEASE)
Address _____

_____   Signature _____

Postcode _____

To Susan Welland
Reader Service
FREEPOST
P.O. Box 236
CROYDON
Surrey CR9 9EL

NO
STAMP
NEEDED

SEND NO MONEY NOW

just Philip Ashborne left, he was the last of his line,
living all alone there in that great house. It seemed sort
of——'

'Romantic?' suggested Jay drily, as she briefly paused.
'Charlotte, you're full of surprises. Ever since I met you,
you've been hardworking and thoroughly practical. I
never realised you had a streak of romance buried deep
inside you.'

'No one sees it very often,' she admitted. 'Sometimes
I even forget it's there.'

'I won't forget,' he promised softly. 'But keep going.
Tell me more about Ashborne Hall.'

'I drove out to see it one afternoon. It was several
miles outside Manchester, and quite near the main road,
yet you couldn't even see it until you were nearly on top
of it. It was a filthy day, pouring with rain, and the grey
stone of the house looked exactly the same colour as the
sky. I sat in the car for a while, staring at the house and
thinking what a depressing place it must be to live in,
despite its age and all its history. Then the front door
opened, and I could see someone standing there. I'd been
planning to telephone, to ask for an interview, but I decided I might as well ask in person, since there was obviously someone at home. I dashed up the steps, and
arrived at the front entrance looking like a drowned rat.
The rain was still belting down, and I just stood there,
dripping with water and wishing this man would ask me
in instead of simply staring at me as if I'd arrived from
another planet.'

'Was it Philip Ashborne?' Jay asked quietly.

Charlie nodded reluctantly. 'I didn't realise that, at
first. I thought he must be the butler, or someone like
that. Eventually, he muttered something about me
coming in, so I scuttled inside. Then I just stood there
and stared. It was like stepping into a palace. Polished
marble, huge gilt-edged mirrors, crystal chandeliers,

these incredible paintings—very different from the poky
little flat where my mother and I had lived for the past
few years! Then I realised that, while I was looking
around with my mouth hanging open, the man who had
let me in was staring at *me*. A bit late in the day, I remembered my manners. I introduced myself and started
to explain why I was there, but he just cut me short. He
said he was Philip Ashborne, then he asked me if I would
have dinner with him that evening. I didn't know what
to say, because it was about the last thing I'd been
expecting. I suppose I must have eventually nodded, because he immediately looked pleased. And that was how
it all began.'

'You must have made quite an impression on him,'
Jay commented.

'I don't know why,' Charlie said with a baffled frown.
'I told you, I was absolutely drenched, with my hair
hanging down like a lot of rats' tails. Afterwards, Philip
said——' She paused, swallowed hard. 'He said it was
love at first sight,' she finally got out in a small voice.
'The moment he saw me, he knew I was the one he
wanted.'

'And how did you feel about it?' asked Jay in an even
voice. 'Was it a two-way thing, were you as bowled over
as he was?'

Charlie shrugged unhappily. 'For the first few days,
I was totally confused. It was like stepping into another
world, I started to feel like Cinderella. I told you, my
mother and I lived in this tiny little flat. And the area
was nothing to write home about, definitely not one of
the up-market parts of Manchester. As long as I could
remember, money had been short, and luxuries were few
and far between. Then, suddenly, there was Philip,
drawing up outside the flat in this huge black Daimler,
and whisking me off to the sort of restaurant where the
price of the meal would have paid the rent on our flat

for a whole month. And Philip himself was quite some-thing to look at. Very tall, very elegant, with pale blond hair and beautiful grey eyes that looked almost silver at times. None of it seemed *real*. I kept thinking I'd wake up and find the whole thing had been a pleasant but bizarre dream.'

'It was real, though.'

'Oh yes, it was real,' she agreed, with some bitterness. 'That fact finally dawned on me the day Philip asked me to marry him.'

Jay's grip on her hand tightened almost perceptibly. 'How long had you known him by then?'

'Only a few weeks. He said he had been sure from the very start, though; that he'd only waited this long to give me a chance to get to know him better.' At that, her mouth twisted into an acid smile. 'Do you want to hear something funny? I thought that I really *did* know him by then.'

'And did you love him?'

His softly spoken question made her search hard for an honest answer. 'I don't know,' she confessed at last. Then she realised what he was really asking, and her blue eyes instantly went icy. 'You think I married him for his money?' she demanded. 'Do you really believe I could do something like that?'

Jay lightly raised his eyebrows. 'You've just told me you were dazzled by all that money and luxury. A lot of girls would have given just about anything for the sort of life-style he was offering you.'

'Not me!' Charlie insisted immediately and vehemently.

'But if you didn't love him——' Jay said pointedly.

'I didn't say that. Only that I wasn't sure. I was cer-tainly fond of him—very fond. In the end, I think it was my mother who finally helped me to decide. We had a long talk, and she told me how much she had loved my father—yet look how that had turned out. He'd run out on her after a couple of years, leaving her with a child to raise all on her own. She reckoned that friendship and affection were a much better basis for marriage in the long term, that love could grow out of those two things, given half a chance. The other type of love—the kind she'd felt for my father—had a habit of burning itself out. It was best to leave it alone, if you had a choice.'

'And you agreed with her?'

'My mother was a very practical woman—she'd had to be, under the circumstances,' Charlie said defensively. 'And she'd brought me up to be the same. What she said made a lot of sense.'

'So you ignored the romantic streak that you never let anyone else see, and decided to accept Philip's proposal?'

'It seemed like the best thing to do, especially since I knew it would work out well for my mother. She'd recently met a rather special man, a Canadian—remember, I told you about him? He was returning to Canada, and he wanted her to go with him, but I knew she wouldn't leave me on my own. If I was married, though, I knew she could go off with a clear conscience. I reckoned it was about time she had a life of her own, after spending all those years bringing me up. Oh, it wasn't the main reason I accepted Philip's proposal,' Charlie went on, 'but it was one more thing that helped to tip the balance in his favour. And I think I was more than fond of Philip by that time, that I was already starting to fall in love with him. I was certainly looking forward to sharing my life with him, getting to know him even better, growing to love him even more. So, next time he asked me to marry him, I said yes. Philip made all the arrangements, and a couple of weeks later the wedding went ahead.' She suddenly stopped talking;

her mouth had gone horribly dry, and she could feel herself beginning to shake.

'All right,' said Jay in an even voice, 'that's the easy bit over with. Now we get to the hard part.' He gave her a brief shake. 'Don't give up now you've got this far. Come on, Charlotte! *Keep talking.*'

CHAPTER SIX

ALMOST automatically, Charlie obeyed him, her tone dull now, as if it were easier to get the words out if she stayed completely unemotional.

'It was a fantastic wedding. The men were all in top hat and tails, there was a horse-drawn carriage to take me to the church, and I wore this incredible hand-made dress in pure silk. All paid for by Philip, of course. He insisted everything had to be absolutely perfect—and it was. Afterwards, we flew to Venice for the honeymoon. Where else but the most romantic city in the world?' she asked, with a sudden wave of cynicism. Then her voice altered again, and went back to its low monotone. 'Perhaps Philip thought it would work some sort of miracle, that some of its magic would rub off on us— on him,' she added heavily.

'Things didn't work out well?' Jay guessed quietly.

Her eyes became dark with remembered pain. 'Things didn't work out at all. Everything was fine until the actual wedding night, but then it all started to fall apart. It turned into a total fiasco. No matter how hard Philip tried, nothing happened—you know what I mean?' she muttered, in a slightly embarrassed voice.

'It's all right,' Jay assured her quickly, 'you don't have to put it into clinical terms. I get the message.'

'At first, I couldn't believe it. It had all been so perfect up until then, and I'd been certain the honeymoon would turn out to be just as marvellous. It never occurred to me that anything could go wrong. Philip had always seemed so sure of himself, so in control of everything—

I'd thought that side of our marriage would be as good as everything else. When it all went wrong, I didn't know what to do. During the day, he wouldn't even talk about it, he just behaved as if everything was fine. And I didn't dare bring the subject up in case it made things worse. I started to feel confused, upset, even a bit resentful. After all, this was meant to be one of life's great experiences, and it had all turned out to be a complete non-event. I was ashamed of feeling that way, because I knew it must be far more humiliating for Philip than it was for me, but I couldn't help it. I had this awful sense of being let down. There had been that fairy-tale courtship, the fantastic wedding—then nothing.'

'How old were you?' asked Jay.

'How old?' she repeated, with a faint frown. 'Nineteen. And I suppose I was a bit immature for my age—although I've certainly made up for it since then,' she added bitterly. 'Why do you want to know?'

'Impotence is a hard thing for a woman to understand and cope with at any age,' he answered, after a brief pause. 'No nineteen-year-old should be expected to deal with it. The man had no right to marry you if he was having those sort of problems. At the very least, he should have confided in you beforehand, told you what to expect, so you knew what you'd be facing if you married him.'

Charlie slowly shook her head. 'Philip could never have done anything like that. He had too much pride. It didn't take me long to find out that he could never talk about anything deeply personal.'

'Didn't it occur to you that you could get an annulment?'

'For those first few days, I couldn't think of anything at all,' she answered rather shakily. 'Then it dawned on me that I was being pretty selfish, that it was every bit as bad for Philip as it was for me. Worse, in fact, be-

cause I wasn't totally naive, I knew how awful it must
be for a man to fail like that. I went for a long walk one
evening and thought the whole thing over very carefully.
Eventually I decided it was something we could work
out in time. There wasn't any rush, we had the whole
of our lives to get it right. I was sure there were doctors
who could help, give advice, and I decided to go and
see one when we got back home. I knew that I needed
to find out more about it, see if there was anything *I*
could do to help put things right. I wouldn't be able to
tell Philip where I'd been, of course, because I knew
how he'd hate it if he ever found out that I'd tried to
get professional advice, but it seemed like the only sensible way to tackle the problem.'

'That was a good decision,' confirmed Jay, with a brief
nod. 'These things hardly ever put themselves right
without expert help. Did you get the advice you needed?'

Charlie stared at the ground. 'There wasn't time,' she
got out at last, each word being reluctantly dragged out
of her now, because she was getting to the part she had
fought so fiercely to forget. All the old memories were
starting to surge over her now, though. She had started
to shake, but she couldn't stop them forcing their way
back into her mind. 'When I got back to the hotel room
after my walk, Philip was waiting for me. And he was
blazingly angry.' She gave a brief shiver. 'I'd never seen
him lose his temper before, he'd always seemed so cool
and controlled until then. He started to fling all these
wild accusations at me. He said that he knew I'd gone
out to meet someone else, that I'd been looking for
someone who would give me what—what he hadn't been
able to.' Her mouth set in a tense line. 'He looked almost
like a stranger, his face was all flushed and his eyes were
nearly black. I was angry at first, when he began to say
all those awful things to me, but finally I started to get
scared as well. He came over and grabbed hold of me,

and I thought he was going to shake me. He didn't, though. That wasn't what he had in mind at all. Getting himself into such a furious temper had somehow unlocked something inside him, he was—aroused,' she went on, almost in a whisper. 'He picked me up and more or less threw me on to the bed. Then he finally managed to—to make love to me.'

Jay's face had darkened perceptibly. 'Did he hurt you?' he asked in a taut voice.

'Yes,' Charlie answered simply. Then she lifted her head a little. 'But it was all over so quickly that it wasn't too bad. And, afterwards, I started to feel almost a sense of relief. I thought things would get better now that he had actually managed to behave like a proper husband, that this would be the real beginning to our marriage.'

'You stupid little innocent!' Jay told her roughly. 'You don't know much about men, do you?'

'I didn't then,' she confirmed, with a small shudder. 'I know a whole lot more now.'

'You should have cleared out that first morning. Just packed your things and walked straight out the door.'

Charlie stared at him with sudden fierceness. 'How could I have done that? I was *married* to Philip. For better, for worse,' she reminded him, flinging the words from the marriage service at him with some bitterness. 'OK, so things weren't so good, but that didn't give me the right to walk out at the first sign of trouble. I knew I had to stay and at least try to put things right.'

Jay gave an impatient shake of his head. 'Any expert would have told you that a man's sexual response is programmed into him quite early on in life, and that it hardly ever changes. If Philip Ashborne could only make love to you when he was worked up and angry, then it was *always* going to be like that.'

'Well, there weren't any experts around at the time to give me that useful piece of advice!' Charlie retorted angrily.

'Then common sense should have told you that you were in way over your head, that you'd got yourself into a situation that you couldn't possibly deal with.' Jay stopped, took a long, slow breath, and then exhaled softly. 'All right, let's cool it,' he said at last. 'I don't want to upset you, I just want to know what happened next. Can you face telling me?'

Charlie twisted her fingers together. 'I suppose so,' she muttered. She hesitated for a few more moments, then finally went on. 'You were right about one thing— it didn't get any better. It just seemed to keep getting worse. Philip would go for ages without touching me, then he'd get into a blazing temper over some silly little thing, and when he was practically beside himself with rage, he'd——' She gave a small shudder. 'Well, I guess you can figure out for yourself what happened.'

Jay nodded briefly, but said nothing, as if he didn't quite trust himself to speak.

'When it was over, he would be full of apologies. He always promised over and over it would never happen again, not like that,' she said, rather wearily. 'At first, I believed him. He seemed so genuinely upset—sometimes he was practically crying. And I think he *did* mean it, at the time. It was just that he wasn't capable of keeping his promise, something inside him wouldn't let him.'

'Did he ever hit you?' Jay asked quietly.

After a brief pause, she reluctantly nodded. 'Not always. But sometimes he did. And afterwards he'd buy me incredibly expensive presents. I suppose he was trying to make up for it. You see, the awful part was that he really did love me. I know it sounds crazy, but it's true. He'd have given me anything I asked for. He used to look at me and I could see the love in his eyes. If it hadn't been for that—that other side of him, I think we could have been really happy together.'

'How long did you put up with it?'

'Six months,' she admitted, her face twisting into a painful grimace. 'Looking back, I suppose I must have been mad to have stuck it for that long, but at times I felt so dreadfully sorry for him. He really hated himself for the way he was behaving, but at the same time he just couldn't stop himself. And he refused to get help. I'd only got to suggest it and he'd practically explode with temper. Since I soon learnt what those bouts of temper led to, after a few weeks I avoided the whole subject like the plague!'

'So what made you finally decide you couldn't take it any longer?' asked Jay in a taut voice.

Charlie shrugged. 'I don't really know. Something inside me just seemed to snap. I knew that, if I stayed much longer, I'd end up as crazy as he was. Because he was a little insane,' she went on evenly. 'I'm pretty sure of that. He was like two people. There was the man I'd married, who was charming, good company, even loving, the sort of person it was very easy to care for. Then there was the other side of him, the dark side, that just flashed out from nowhere and seemed to take over completely, making him do all those disgusting things. I suppose a psychiatrist might have been able to explain it, perhaps even been able to help him, but there was no way Philip would ever have agreed to see one. He wouldn't even admit he had a problem.'

'It sounds like a sort of schizophrenia,' Jay said rather grimly. 'How did he take it when you told him you were leaving?'

'I didn't tell him. I was too scared by then. I didn't know how he'd react—what he'd do. I just waited until he'd gone out, then I packed my things and rang for a taxi. I thought I could be miles away by the time Philip finally returned home.'

'But it didn't work out like that?' queried Jay, with a dark frown.

'No,' she said very softly. 'He'd forgotten some important papers, and he came back to get them. He found me in the bedroom, finishing the last of my packing.' She shivered violently. 'He guessed at once what was happening, and his face changed so completely, he looked—awful. God, I was scared!' she recalled, with another bleak shiver. 'He just stood there and stared at me for absolutely ages, and I couldn't move, I couldn't even say anything. Then he reached into his pocket and took out this penknife.' Jay swore quietly but vehemently under his breath, then fell silent again, waiting tensely for her to go on. 'I thought he was going to kill me,' Charlie admitted tightly. 'All of a sudden he moved—he grabbed me and threw me down on to the bed. His eyes were so wild, and his face was bright red and dripping with sweat. He tore off my blouse, and I could feel the edge of the knife against my skin. It was so cold——'

Her voice began to shake. She tried to steady it, but couldn't because the vivid pictures were racing through her head now; it was like living through the whole horrific scene all over again. 'Then the blade was cutting into my skin, and it was funny but it didn't really hurt, but I could feel the blood and I was sure I was going to die. After a while he stopped, though; then he just looked down at me with this really weird glow in his eyes. "Now everyone will know you belong to me," he said, and it wasn't until afterwards that I found he'd carved his initials on to my skin, like someone permanently branding one of their possessions.' She shook her head despairingly. 'How could anyone do something like that?'

'They couldn't,' confirmed Jay grimly, 'not unless they were insane.'

'That wasn't the end of it, though,' she told him through gritted teeth. 'The knife started to dig into me again, and this time he was holding it right over my heart. I was so damned *terrified*! He was completely out of control by this time; looking into his eyes was like looking right into some tormented kind of hell. He was capable of just about anything at that moment.'

'Wasn't there anyone else in the house?' asked Jay tightly. 'You must have had some sort of domestic staff, you couldn't have looked after a place that size single-handedly.'

'There was a housekeeper, but it was her day off. And a couple of local women came in the mornings, to help with the cleaning and polishing, but they'd already left. We were on our own, I knew no one was going to come dashing in to help. I thought it was the end, and it was odd but it was almost a relief. I couldn't face another day of living under that awful strain, and I knew now he was never going to let me go. I could run and run, but I'd never get away from him, he'd always come after me and find me. I didn't *want* to die, but the alternative was pretty appalling. Anyway, it didn't seem I was going to get a choice. I remember closing my eyes and praying it wouldn't be too painful; then I started hearing this ringing in my ears. I thought I was passing out, and I was really grateful for that. I'd reached the stage where I just couldn't stand another second of what was happening. But I didn't faint and the ringing went on and on. Philip seemed to have gone very still and quiet, and it finally dawned on me that the ringing wasn't inside my head, I was actually hearing it. It was the doorbell. Then I remembered I'd phoned earlier for a taxi. I realised it must be the driver downstairs, pressing hard on the bell, trying to make someone hear.'

'What did Philip do?'

'For what seemed like ages, he didn't do anything at all,' she recalled, her face pale now, and her eyes heavy and dark with strain. 'He just lay there beside me on the bed, staring down at me—and at the blood on my skin, on the sheets. Then his eyes began to clear, all that dreadful wildness just melted away. Instead, he began to look totally horrified, as if he was just starting to realise what he'd done—and how much further he'd have gone, if that doorbell hadn't rung. I'd never seen him look so awful. For a moment, I almost felt sorry for him. I started to say something, but he didn't listen, he just flung himself off the bed and ran straight out of the room. A minute later, I heard his car revving up and driving off at top speed.'

'Did you get out of there, while you had the chance?' Jay asked, his own features deeply shadowed now.

'I didn't do anything,' Charlie said numbly. 'I just lay there. I felt too shocked and ill to move, even to think. I heard the taxi driver finally leave, then it was very quiet, the house seemed like a morgue. And I was cold, I re-member feeling terribly cold, but I couldn't even find enough energy to drag the quilt over me. Eventually, it started to get dark, and some time after that I heard a car pulling up outside. I thought it was Philip coming back again, but somehow I didn't care. I'd gone way past the stage where anything seemed to matter any more. It wasn't Philip, though—it was the police. They'd come to tell me about the accident. Philip's car had skidded off the road just a couple of miles from Ashborne Hall. He had been killed instantly——'

As her voice trailed away, Jay shot a sharp glance at her. 'Suicide?' he said bluntly.

'I don't know.' She gave a helpless shrug. 'They couldn't find anything wrong with the car, but there had been a heavy shower of rain, and the road was wet and rather greasy. They eventually recorded a verdict of accidental death. Did he mean to kill himself? I don't know!' she repeated with a touch of despair. 'I wish I did. It might have made me feel better.'

'Made *you* feel better?' repeated Jay, a note of disbelief colouring his voice. 'Why the hell should you have felt bad about what happened?'

'Stupid, isn't it?' she said colourlessly. 'But I've always felt as if I failed him; that there should have been something I could have done to put things right between us, stop it all happening the way it did.'

'If you think that, you're as crazy as he was,' Jay said without compunction. 'The man had serious mental problems. Even an experienced psychiatrist might not have been able to straighten him out.'

'I know that,' agreed Charlie tiredly. 'If I look at the whole thing logically, I *know* it wasn't my fault, not even the—the way he died,' she finished falteringly. 'But I can't help the way I feel inside. There's this huge lump of guilt that sometimes just swells up bigger and bigger, until I feel as if I'm choking on it. And do you know what makes it worse?' When Jay slowly shook his head, she went on, 'Philip left me everything. The house, all the fabulous treasures in it, huge holdings of stocks and shares, his entire income—it was all mine.'

'What did you do with it?'

'Nothing! I haven't touched a single penny of it. I couldn't, it's like—like blood money,' Charlie said with a deep shudder. 'There's a firm of solicitors who look after the estate. I don't want anything to do with it.'

'Talking of blood,' said Jay slowly, 'didn't the police notice anything suspicious when they came to the house, to tell you about the accident? You must have been in a bad state, and there were all those cuts on your skin.'

'I covered myself up before I went down to let them in,' Charlie answered dully. 'I'd stopped bleeding by then—the cuts hadn't been very deep, thank God. I suppose I must have looked a bit odd, but they probably put that down to the shock of hearing about Philip's death.'

Jay suddenly looked at her piercingly. 'Why the hell have you kept all this bottled up inside you all this time? Damn it, Charlotte,' he went on tautly, 'you're not stupid! You must have known that was the worst possible thing you could have done.'

'And who was I supposed to talk to?' she challenged, rounding on him angrily. 'The police? What was the point? They could hardly have pressed charges for assault—Philip was *dead*. And what if the newspapers had got hold of the story? Do you think I could have stood seeing it splashed right across the front pages?'

'What about your mother?' Jay said tightly. 'Surely you could have told her?'

'She flew back from Canada for the funeral,' Charlie answered, calming down a little again, 'but it was pretty obvious she couldn't wait to get back. She was having a great time over there, and I didn't want to spoil it for her. She'd had a rough few years while she was bringing me up single-handedly, and I figured she deserved whatever happiness she could get. If I'd confided in her, told her what the last six months had really been like, she'd have insisted on staying. Instead, I just said that the marriage hadn't been working out too well, so I wasn't completely heartbroken over Philip's death. I told her I was planning to move down to London, to start a new life for myself, and there was absolutely no need for her to worry about me.'

'And she swallowed that story?'

Charlie somehow managed a very faint smile. 'I can be a very convincing liar, when I put my mind to it.'

But Jay was looking at her with new thoughtfulness now. 'So I'm the first person to whom you've ever told the whole story?'

'Well—yes,' she admitted reluctantly.

'Why me?'

'I don't know. I didn't *want* to tell you,' she reminded him. 'But once I'd started—I couldn't seem to stop,' she finished with a fast growing sense of awkwardness.

'And how do you feel now?'

'What do you mean?'

Jay smiled a trifle grimly. 'You know exactly what I mean. So be honest with me, Charlotte.'

But she was already regretting that she had blurted out all those painfully personal and intimate details. It made her feel far too vulnerable. This man knew things about her that no one else on this earth knew about. She wasn't at all sure that she liked that. It was a very uncomfortable sensation, as if he had somehow managed to burrow right inside her skin. And, anyway, she didn't want to talk any more. She felt totally empty inside, as if there just weren't any words, any thoughts, any emotions left in her.

'All I feel right now is tired,' she muttered defensively, after a long silence. 'And my hand still hurts where that damned ant bit it. I think I'll go and lie down for a while, have a rest.'

She waited tensely for him to try and stop her, but to her surprise—and utter relief—he didn't make any attempt to detain her. It was as if he instinctively realised that she rather desperately needed to be on her own for a while.

Stumbling over to the hut she made her way inside; then she collapsed into the hammock. Her heart seemed to be thudding much harder and faster than usual, but for the first time in three years her head seemed free of its heavy burden of horrific memories. She closed her eyes tiredly, and, against all expectations, almost instantly slid into a deep, dreamless sleep.

Charlie slept until early in the afternoon; then she got up and made herself something to eat, surprised to find that her appetite was quite good. For the rest of the day, she just lazed around. Although Jay always remained within sight, as if silently telling her that he was there if she needed him, he left her very much alone, and for that she was grateful. Once evening closed in, she crawled back into the hammock, and was soon sound asleep again, as if her body craved all the rest it could get.

Next morning, she woke up feeling relaxed and astonishingly full of energy. Whenever she allowed herself to think about yesterday, she could hardly believe she had actually told Jay so much of the dark secret she had hoarded within herself these past three years. In the end, she forced herself to stop thinking about it, putting it firmly out of her mind. If she kept brooding over it, she knew she would just get nervous and worked up, wondering what—if anything—he intended to do about it.

She got out the portable typewriter, set it up on the folding table, then sorted out her folders of papers. Right at the bottom was the file with the notes she had started to make for her article on Jay Challoner. For a few seconds, she simply stared at them, as if they had been written by someone else. For the last couple of days, she had hardly given a thought to the real reason she was here. London—Dan Marshall—*Tomorrow* magazine— they all seemed a million miles away, nothing at all to do with the life she was leading here in this hot, damp corner of the rain forest.

Carry on thinking along those lines, and Dan Marshall will start looking for someone else to do your job, she told herself tartly. When she had got a free hour, she would definitely make a serious start on her article. It was about time she hauled herself back into the real world. She had started to get far too self-absorbed and introspective these last few days.

She had just wound the first sheet of paper into the typewriter when Jay ambled over. To her annoyance, she found herself flushing slightly, and she kept her gaze glued to the paper, refusing to look up at him.

'You can't ignore me for ever,' he told her, a faint note of amusement in his voice.

'I'm not ignoring you,' she insisted with some dignity. 'I just don't want—well, don't want to——'

'To look at me?' Jay finished for her, as she floundered slightly, searching for the right words.

Charlie's tense facial muscles relaxed into a reluctant grin. 'I suppose so,' she admitted. 'I know it's silly, but I feel sort of—embarrassed.'

'Because of what you told me yesterday?'

She nodded. 'You know—too much about me.'

He settled himself comfortably down beside her. 'I know what happened to you three years ago. I know why you don't like me—or any other man—touching you. But we've still got a long way to go, Charlotte. We've only just begun to find out about each other.'

At that, she finally raised her head and looked at him, her blue gaze locking warily on to his own bi-coloured eyes. 'What do you mean?' she asked in a guarded tone.

'So far, we've done little more than get a few basic facts straightened out.'

'A few basic facts?' she echoed incredulously. 'But I told you——' Hurriedly, she shut up. She didn't want to remember what she had told him.

'It was a useful start,' Jay agreed, and she had the impression that he was deliberately keeping his voice light and casual, not letting the conversation get too serious—at least, not yet. 'For instance, I know that you're not after my money,' he teased her lightly. 'You're a very wealthy lady in your own right.'

'I'll never touch a penny of Philip's money! Never!' she shot back instantly.

'Then what are you going to do with it? And what about the house, Ashborne Hall? From what you've told me, it's chock-a-block with priceless treasures. Do you think it's right to just leave them there to rot?'

'The solicitors have made very adequate arrangements for the upkeep of the house,' she told him furiously. 'Not that it's any affair of yours!'

He refused to be riled. 'Are you sure you're never going to want to live there again?'

Just the thought of it made Charlie shiver. 'Definitely not,' she said vehemently.

'Then why not turn it over to an institution such as the National Trust, or some similar organisation? It would be an ideal way of getting rid of it, yet at the same time you'd be making sure that the house and its treasures were kept intact for future generations to enjoy. And it would solve the problem of what to do with all that money Philip left you. It could be channelled into a fund that would provide enough income for the upkeep of the house. I believe the National Trust won't accept properties without that kind of financial provision.'

Charlie simply stared at him, her flare of temper completely forgotten. Why hadn't she ever thought of such a simple solution? Ashborne Hall and Philip's money could be disposed of at a single stroke! And she wouldn't have to feel guilty about getting rid of the house, because the Hall and its treasures would be looked after efficiently and expertly. She was sure Philip would have approved of such an arrangement.

'I'll get in touch with the solicitors when I get back to London,' she said slowly. 'They'll be able to find out if the whole thing's possible.'

'I shouldn't think you'll run into any major diffi-
culties,' said Jay easily. 'Now we've settled that problem,
there's another—and rather more urgent—matter to be
dealt with. You're not going to like it, so we'd better get
it over with. Then you can relax for the rest of the day.'

'What is it?' Charlie asked cautiously.

'Remember how I told you we'd have to check each
other regularly for any sign of parasite infestation?' As
she gave a disbelieving groan, he nodded. 'That's right.
It's time for another check-up. I know it's bad timing,
springing this on you right on top of all yesterday's
traumas, but we've already left it too long. Ideally, we
should go through this routine every couple of days, and
it's nearly a week since we checked each other over. Do
you think you can face it?'

She was about to tell him that she definitely couldn't,
that it was about the last thing on earth she felt like right
now, when she suddenly stopped. All right, so she wasn't
exactly thrilled by the prospect. On the other hand, she
wasn't completely panicking at the mere thought of it;
his suggestion hadn't instantly filled her with all the old,
haunting sense of horror. Which was surprising—*very*
surprising.

'I suppose, if it's really essential, we'd better go
through with it,' she conceded at last, still faintly astonished that she hadn't felt the need to put up more of
a fight against it.

Jay gave a nod of approval, and Charlie felt an unexpected glow inside her, as if a part of her was pleased
that he approved of—even admired—the way she was
facing up to all the problems and obstacles that kept
looming up in front of her.

'Shall I go first?' asked Jay. Without waiting for her
reply, he stripped off without the slightest trace of embarrassment; then he sprawled out beside her, lying on
his stomach.

Since he didn't always bother to wear a shirt, his skin was more tanned than last time, and it glowed with health. Charlie couldn't help comparing Jay's body with Philip's, which had always looked rather pale and somehow lifeless, as if he rarely exposed himself to the sun and fresh air. Her gaze slid over the well defined muscles, the strong line of Jay's back, and then rather hurriedly skipped over the long, powerful set of his thighs.

'You can touch me, if you like,' Jay said in a rather lazy voice.

She was instantly on her guard. 'Why should I want to do that?'

He gave a casual shrug. 'Just to see what happens.'

And the incredible thing was that she really was tempted. The tips of her fingers had actually begun to twitch involuntarily, as if they could hardly wait to try out such a daring experiment.

Charlie sat up rather primly, firmly locking her hands together in her lap, as if she didn't entirely trust them any more. 'I don't think that would be a good idea.'

'Why not?' And there was a slightly husky, almost an inviting note in Jay's voice now.

She knew he couldn't see her. He was still lying on his stomach, with his face resting against one outflung arm. All the same, she couldn't quite get rid of the disturbing impression that he was very much aware of the half-nervous, half-anticipatory look that hovered over her face.

'Admit it—you *want* to give it a try,' he went on softly, coaxingly. 'So why not have the guts to go for it? Or are you too scared, Charlotte?' he challenged.

'Of course I'm damned well scared!' she retorted edgily. 'What if——' She drew in a deep breath. 'What if it's just as bad as it was before?'

'How are you going to know if you won't put it to the test?'

'I suppose I won't,' Charlie admitted with a lot of reluctance. 'I just wish—well, that it didn't have to be so soon. That it didn't have to be *now*.'

'What do you want to do? Put if off for another day? Another week? Or indefinitely?' he goaded her gently.

She took a deep breath. He was right, of course. But then, he was always right! she told herself with a fresh rush of irritation. He seemed to know exactly when to push her, and when to hold back and let things ride for a while, until she was in a better frame of mind. Look at the way he had handled yesterday's crisis; expertly leading her on until she had finally got the whole thing out of her system, then leaving her alone, giving her space, so she'd have a chance to get over that mental purging in her own time. It made her feel—well, sort of safe when he was around, she conceded. As if she could always trust him to do the right thing at exactly the right time. And she wasn't sure she liked that. Jay Challoner could certainly be a real pussycat when he put his mind to it, but Charlie wasn't fooled for a moment. There was a very different type of animal lurking behind those alert, all-seeing eyes. Right now, he might look as relaxed and unthreatening as a lion who's just eaten a huge meal and feels too lethargic to move a single muscle. That didn't mean he couldn't pounce dangerously, though, if he suddenly decided to put his mind to it. And Charlie couldn't quite banish a niggling sense of deep unease. After all, what did he want from her? Why had he gone to so much trouble over the last few days to try and put things right for her? What was he expecting in return?

With an effort, she pushed all the unsettling questions out of her mind. There was only one question she had to answer right now—did she want to risk touching him, or not?

She stared down at his prone body. How did she really feel about it? Not too bad, she realised with some surprise. As bodies went, this was definitely a pretty impressive specimen. Hard and powerful, well proportioned—if she had any artistic tendencies, she would probably be itching to draw or sculpt those marvellously perfect lines.

'You can't put it off for ever,' Jay reminded her quietly. 'So, how about it, Charlotte? Have you got the guts to give it a try?'

'I suppose so,' she said reluctantly. Then she added anxiously, 'You won't move?'

'Not a muscle,' he promised. 'Not unless you want me to.'

'I won't,' she assured him hurriedly. Then she nervously flexed her fingers, trying to convince herself that this was no big deal. She was only going to *touch* him, for heaven's sake! If all the old feelings of revulsion rushed over her, all she had to do was let go again and walk away. She wasn't committing herself to anything, so she might as well go ahead and get it over with right now, before her already shaky nerves gave way completely...

With a jerky movement, she reached out and gingerly rested her palm on the small of his back. Then she somehow forced herself to let it stay there.

'How does it feel?' asked Jay a few seconds later.

'It's—all right,' she admitted, a faint note of astonishment creeping into her voice.

She wasn't lying, either. His skin was warm and smooth against her palm. She was almost enjoying the pleasant tactile sensation.

'Want to try something a little more adventurous?'

Charlie wasn't sure that she did, but there had been a definite note of challenge in his voice this time, and she couldn't stop herself from responding to it. Cautiously, she slid her hand up towards his shoulders. Her fingers almost involuntarily began to explore the outline of the strong muscles just below the surface of that silky, slightly damp skin, and she felt her hand begin to tingle slightly, as if some automatic response had been triggered in her own nervous system.

'Very nice,' murmured Jay. 'Keep it up for as long as you like.'

Charlie blinked. 'You're enjoying it?'

He half turned his head so that one eye—the blue one—was now looking up at her.

'Did you think I wouldn't?' he responded, with some amusement. 'Most men enjoy being touched by a beautiful girl. There's nothing unusual or perverse about that.'

'But I thought——' she began nervously.

The blue eye gazed up at her speculatively. 'You thought what?'

'Well—I thought that—damn it, you know what I thought!' Charlie spluttered at last.

Jay grinned. 'That from my point of view this was just an interesting piece of research? That I was approaching the whole thing cold-bloodedly, not letting myself get involved?'

'Something like that,' she admitted, her insides fluttering wildly now with unease.

His grin broadened. 'Wrong, Charlotte. Don't worry,' he went on, seeing the alarm beginning to spread over her face. 'I'll keep a tight grip on things. You needn't worry that any of this will get out of control. But I'm definitely having a great time—and I intend to go on enjoying it. So—do you want to carry on, or are you going to panic and run away?'

She wasn't sure. None of this was turning out at all as she had expected.

'I suppose I'll carry on,' she said edgily, at last. 'Just for a little while longer.'

She let her hand slide slowly back to his waist, but then decided that it might be better to quit while she was ahead. As soon as she lifted her hand away, though, she was swept by a giddily disturbing urge to put it right back again, and she blinked hard in pure amazement.

'Did you see any sign of parasite bites on my back?' asked Jay.

'Oh—no—I don't think so,' Charlie gabbled in confusion. The truth was, she had forgotten to look! The touch of his skin had so fascinated her that she had been totally absorbed by it. Hurriedly, she scanned his skin, but couldn't see any red or inflamed marks. 'No, you're quite clear.'

'Fine. Then I think it's time we changed places.'

With fumbling fingers, she took off her blouse and slipped out of her shorts. Then she saw Jay's features briefly darken as his gaze rested on the faint pattern of scars on her chest. Instinctively, she covered them with her hands. He immediately reached out, though, closing his fingers over her own and then firmly pulling them away.

'Bloody maniac!' he muttered under his breath as his eyes scanned the thin white lines. Then, in a more even tone of voice, 'A good plastic surgeon would be able to get rid of those scars for you.'

'Even if I couldn't see them any more, I'd still know they were there,' Charlie answered in a low voice. Then she raised her head and looked straight at him. 'Do they bother you?'

Jay stared back at her steadily. 'Do you think I'm the sort of man who would be bothered by a few marks on your skin?'

No, she didn't. She had only asked the question because, for some reason, she had needed to hear him actually say it out loud. He let go of her hands and, without another word, she stretched out on her stomach beside him.

She had known all along that he didn't intend to just look at her, and she had thought she was prepared for what would happen next. All the same, she still jumped when she felt that first contact of his hand against her skin. Jay was instantly aware of her reaction, and she felt him become quite still. Nervously, she turned her head to look up at him; then she couldn't stop herself shrinking back slightly. He seemed to be looming over her, his shadow swallowing her up and completely blotting out the light.

'What's wrong?' he queried a little roughly.

'Nothing, really,' Charlie mumbled edgily. 'It's just that—well, you're so *big*,' she blurted out.

His eyes narrowed perceptibly. 'And you think I'd use my size, my strength, against you?'

'No, but——' She stopped, then tried again. 'What I think and what I feel—most of the time, they seem to be two entirely different things. I can't seem to match them up.'

'Are you trying to tell me you're scared, because you know you couldn't do anything about it if I decided to force you into the sort of situation that terrifies you?'

'Something like that,' she admitted. 'I mean, I know you wouldn't hurt me, but you still make me nervous. Silly, isn't it?'

Jay shook his head. 'Not silly. But it means you've still got a lot of mixed-up thoughts inside that gorgeous head of yours. So let's see what we can do about getting rid of them.'

His hand returned to her back, more firmly this time, and she somehow managed not to flinch. It wasn't as difficult as she had expected. In fact, in a remarkably short time she found herself beginning to enjoy the warm brushing of skin against skin. It was unexpectedly soothing, and she felt her muscles slowly starting to relax. After a few minutes of that light, undemanding caressing, she was almost ready to purr with pleasure.

'Everything all right?' asked Jay softly.

'Mmm,' she nodded, almost sleepily. A few more minutes of this and she would be so completely relaxed that she would doze off. If only it could be marketed, it would sell like crazy—a guaranteed cure for insomnia!

Jay's fingers moved smoothly, slowly, up to the nape of her neck. Suddenly, and without any warning, she was wide awake again. The unexpected tingle that had vibrated down her spine had definitely woken her up. Did she like it? She wasn't sure; she thought that she did. Before she had time to reach a definite decision, though, those clever fingers of his were on the move again. They were tickling her ear now, and that felt— well, she didn't know quite how to describe it, except that it wasn't unpleasant. No, not unpleasant at all.

'Turn over,' murmured Jay in a relaxed tone.

Her heavy eyes flickered open. Why did he want her to do that? He only needed to check her back; she could find any parasite bites on her front perfectly well herself. All the same, it was hard to disobey that dark velvet male voice, and she found herself rather lethargically rolling over on to her back.

Then Charlie let out an audible gasp of protest. She hadn't realised he had unhooked her bra! As her breasts slithered free, she rather frantically grabbed for the light wisp of cotton, but Jay's hands got there first. He slid the loose straps down her arms, then whisked it away completely.

Charlie briefly froze. Why did he have to spoil it? Everything had been going so well, but he was like all men! He was greedy, he wanted more than she was willing to give. And if he decided to just take it . . .

'Don't worry,' Jay told her quietly, as if he could read every thought whizzing through her head. 'We're not going too far. Not today.'

'A lot of men say that,' she muttered. 'But, when it comes down to it, they don't—they can't keep their word.'

'Don't confuse me with Philip,' he instructed, his eyes briefly glittering. 'I might get impatient, even a little frustrated, but I won't lose control, I promise you that. Trust me, Charlotte.'

And it was the oddest thing, but she did. He waited until she had begun to relax again; then his hands started the same slow journey of exploration that they had already traced over her back. She caught her breath when his fingers began to follow the lines of the faint white scars on her upper chest, but she didn't try to stop him. And when he bent his head and lightly retraced the same pattern with the warm tip of his tongue, she found her breathing becoming shallow and a little faster. Somehow, his touch was having a very different effect on her this time. She didn't feel sleepy, quite the opposite—something inside her seemed to be stirring restlessly. She didn't know what it was, but she was sure Jay could sense it, too. She could feel an air of satisfaction beginning to radiate out from him. If she asked him, she was sure he would be able to explain exactly what was happening to her, but she didn't want to talk to him right now. In fact, she didn't want to do anything that would distract him from what he was doing at this precise moment.

A few seconds later, Jay paused. Then he lifted his head and looked down at her, as if assessing her mood. She had no idea what he could read in her eyes, but she saw his own gaze darken a little, and she had the distinct impression that he was pleased with what he saw. Then he bent his head a little further and gently kissed the tips of each of her breasts.

The sensation was electric! Charlie felt as if something had just turned molten in the pit of her stomach; she actually gasped out loud.

Jay didn't say a word, though. And, when she finally found the nerve to turn her head and look at him, she was astonished to find he had moved away and had begun to pull on his shirt.

He saw the look of total surprise on her face, and grinned. 'I thought we'd better stop while things were still going well. There's no point in pushing it too fast. But don't worry, Charlotte—we'll definitely come back to this at some other time.'

He finished dressing, then walked away, and Charlie watched him go with troubled eyes. Everything was changing—*she* was changing—and this man was the one who was making it happen. The trouble was, she wasn't at all sure that she liked what was going on. For the first time in three years, she wasn't totally in control of her life. And she needed that control; it was what had kept her going, held everything together. What was going to happen now that Jay had stepped in and taken it away from her?

She gave a small shiver. She knew what the problem was—he was forcing her to trust him. And she had learnt the hard way that it wasn't safe to trust a man. The future was suddenly starting to look frighteningly uncertain, and she wasn't sure her frayed and battered nerves could cope with all the upheavals that she was sure still lay ahead of her.

CHAPTER SEVEN

To CHARLIE'S relief, the next couple of days passed without any major problems. They got quite a lot of work done, and she guessed they must be nearly halfway through Jay's book now. On the second afternoon, the sun blazed down even more fiercely than usual, and they eventually gave up trying to work. Instead, they went for a dip in the river, sticking close to the bank so they wouldn't have any problems with the strong current near the middle. Charlie had been rather wary when Jay had first suggested a swim. Did he have something else in mind as well? But it soon became clear that he didn't. Their swim passed without incident, and he didn't even try to touch her. Afterwards, they sprawled out on the bank and gently steamed dry, and after a while Jay actually fell asleep.

Charlie stared down at him with an illogical mixture of disappointment and peevishness. Well, it hadn't taken him long to lose interest! She should have known he would quickly get bored with her. These last couple of weeks must have seemed very tame after living with the Eskimos, or going through the throes of a red-hot affair in remotest Africa! And to think she had been worried about what he was planning next, where she was concerned. The answer was pretty obvious—nothing! He just wanted to laze his way through the next few days, then hightail it back to civilisation, and all those girls who knew exactly what to do when a man touched them, who didn't cringe every time he laid a finger on them.

She looked away from him and glared irritably at the scene in front of her. Trees, trees, and more trees. And a few brilliantly coloured, noisy birds. She was definitely getting tired of this particular patch of paradise. It rapidly seemed to be losing all of its charm. Insects that bit you, monkeys that you never saw, but that woke you up at some unearthly hour with their howling, a river that looked calm and peaceful, but could easily sweep you away—she was positively pining for the sight of a car, an office block, proper houses, crowds of people hurrying to and from work. This back-to-nature business might be fine for a lot of people, but it definitely wasn't for her!

Still in the grip of the black mood that had swept over her without any warning, Charlie got to her feet and trudged back to the hut. Her hair was dry now, but still tangled after her swim, so she sat and brushed it until it was silky-smooth and gleaming again. Then she got up and mooched around restlessly for a while. It was too hot to do anything, but she couldn't seem to sit still. She wandered back to the hut, then stood in the doorway where there was a patch of shade that gave a little protection from the scorching sun.

A few minutes later, Jay came ambling over, still looking half asleep. Charlie wasn't fooled, though. She was willing to bet that clever brain of his was ticking over at its usual speed behind those sleepy eyes. And she had seen that somnambulant look on a cat's face, just before it pounced. It was intended to lull its prey into a false sense of security. They would take a look at the cat's relaxed, slightly lazy posture, and think they were safe, that it wasn't going to bother with them today. Then, a couple of seconds later, they would find out just how wrong they had been!

But nothing happened; Jay was amiable and friendly in a very casual sort of way, but that was all. Charlie began to feel inexplicably angry all over again. For the last couple of days, she had spent most of her time waiting for him to make a move. And the fact that he hadn't, that he had behaved like a perfect gentleman, was now starting to get on her nerves for some unaccountable reason. She knew she ought to be feeling thoroughly relieved. Instead, though, she was having to fight off steadily deepening waves of pure resentment.

Next time Jay walked past her, she glowered at him darkly. He took no notice, though. She might just as well not have been there. He got an even blacker look on his way back and, when he asked her a casual question a few minutes later, she nearly snapped his head off.

Jay looked at her thoughtfully. 'Get out of your hammock on the wrong side this morning?' he enquired, with a slight lifting of one eyebrow.

'Oh, very funny!' she muttered.

'Then perhaps there's another reason why you've been scowling at me all afternoon,' he suggested.

But she definitely didn't want to have to go into any sort of explanations. In fact, she would have found it hard to have explained even to herself why she was behaving like this. She should be pleased he had stopped interfering in her life, not going around glaring at him absolutely thunderously.

Jay lounged against the thick wooden pole that formed one side of the open doorway. Then he looked at her tense, moody face. 'Do you want to know what I think?'

'Not particularly,' she said stiffly.

'I think I'll tell you, anyway,' he went on in a relaxed tone. 'For the last couple of days, you've been watching me practically every second of the day—and probably the night as well, or at least for as long as you could stay awake. All the time, you were just waiting for me to try and carry on from that very interesting point where we left off.' Charlie opened her mouth to protest ve-

hemently, but then shut it again. What was the point?
He was right, of course. The damned man was always
right! 'Then this afternoon,' Jay continued, 'it suddenly
dawned on you that I might have no intention of
touching you again. That I'd got thoroughly bored with
the whole thing—got bored with *you*. And you were
rather shocked to find that you didn't particularly like
that idea. In fact, the more you thought about it, the
less you liked it. So, instead of being nervous and jumpy,
you got thoroughly angry instead. You're still in a filthy
temper right now. That lovely mouth of yours looks as
if it would be quite happy to spit at me, given half a
chance.'

'You're always so sure that you know exactly what
I'm thinking, what's going on inside me,' Charlie flung
at him resentfully.

'That's probably because I do,' Jay told her, his voice
still perfectly relaxed. 'And, in case you're wondering,
that's a fairly novel sensation for me, too. I don't usually
poke around inside other people's heads—at least, not
without their permission.'

'Well, I wish you'd just stay out of mine,' she retorted. 'I don't like it!'

Jay shrugged. 'I've not got a lot of choice. I can't *help*
knowing what you're feeling, what you're thinking.'

'Since you've set yourself up as an authority on the
subject, I suppose you know exactly what to do next,
to get me out of this mood?'

'I know there are a lot of very confused feelings
churning round inside you,' Jay replied calmly. 'And
the reason's pretty obvious. You've started to want
something that you thought you'd never want again. You
keep fighting it, though. A part of you is still scared of
it, you're not sure you can cope. And so you've started
to get angry. Not with me, but with yourself, because
you don't like being a coward.'

Charlie sniffed loftily. 'The whole thing sounds too complicated for words. Anyway, what is this "something" that I'm scared and angry about, but still want?'

'This,' came Jay's simple response. And, without saying another word, he bent his head and kissed her.

As kisses went, it was hardly an earthshaking event, little more than the light touching of his warm lips against her own. All the same, Charlie had the disturbing impression that the ground beneath her feet had just moved a trifle.

Jay lifted his head and studied her face. 'How was it?'

'All right, I suppose,' she said guardedly. Then she stared up at him in dawning comprehension. 'You've been *deliberately* ignoring me for the last couple of days, haven't you? Winding me up, so I'd finally realise——'

'Realise what?' he prompted softly, as her voice trailed away.

But she couldn't say it, her tongue just wouldn't get the words out. Anyway, it was so incredible that she wasn't even sure she believed it. Miracle cures didn't happen overnight. All the same, she was definitely starting to feel rather funny. Her legs were shaking, she felt sort of hot, slightly breathless, and she knew her face was flushed.

'Realise that you wanted this?' suggested Jay, a trace of colour showing along his own cheekbones, and his eyes much darker than she ever remembered seeing them before.

This time, his kiss was so slow and thorough that she felt sure there wasn't a corner of her mouth he hadn't explored. No one had ever kissed her like this before in her entire life. And the incredible thing was that she didn't hate it; it definitely didn't make her feel ill. In fact, she would have been perfectly happy if it had gone on and on . . .

But after a while Jay raised his head, and once again that brilliant gaze was fixed on her, as if he was carefully gauging her reaction. She wasn't sure she liked that, it was somehow too—well, too clinical, she decided with a wave of unease.

'How was it this time?' he asked.

It occurred to Charlie that it might not be a good idea to get carried away by all this; to let him see that something inside her had started to glow warmly.

'Quite nice,' she answered cautiously, relieved to find that her voice sounded fairly steady and normal.

One of Jay's eyebrows instantly shot up. 'Nice? *Nice*?' he repeated, a little incredulously. 'In that case, I must be losing my touch! Perhaps we'd better try again.'

And there was nothing restrained about his kiss this time: it was hard and deep and demanding, leaving Charlie feeling as if she had just been steamrollered, completely flattened by something that she didn't understand, but that most definitely felt good. No, not good— fantastic! How on earth could she have been scared of something like this? Every part of her seemed to be clamouring for a repeat performance, and she saw Jay give a brief smile of satisfaction before obliging.

It was just as good. In fact, it was almost better, if that were possible. Charlie sighed in pure wonder. What revelations were going to come next? After all, that had been just a kiss; the only parts of them that had been touching were their mouths, and the tips of their fingers as they had lightly linked hands. His big, powerful body was only inches away, though. All she had to do was reach out, and it would be hers to explore. And her palms were suddenly itching to do just that: to slide over the warm, smooth skin that was already familiar to her, brush against the hard muscles, mutely admiring their gentle strength.

But she didn't get a chance; Jay was already backing away from her. Forcing her heavy eyes open, she murmured a protest and then lifted a hand, as if to stop him.

His fingers lightly locked around her wrist. 'That's quite enough for today,' he instructed.

Her whirling head began to clear and she looked up at him a trifle indignantly. 'You're the one who wanted to cure me,' she reminded him. 'And now it looks like you're succeeding, you're starting to back off.'

His mouth was set in a slightly harder line than usual. 'There's a very good reason for that,' he told her, his voice coloured by a deep note of huskiness. 'And, if you gave it a moment's thought, you'd realise what it was.'

Charlie suddenly flushed. 'But you said—you told me——' She stuttered to a slightly embarrassed halt.

'That I wouldn't lose control?' Jay finished for her. 'Don't worry, I won't. But I'm not a saint, Charlotte. And, even if I were, you'd still tempt me. So make sure you back off when I say stop, give me breathing space when I need it.'

'But we only kissed,' she muttered awkwardly.

'Sometimes that's all it takes.' His fingers were still holding her wrist. 'You don't believe me?' he challenged softly. He pulled her hand a little closer. Charlie's eyes flew wide open, and she hurriedly wrenched her fingers free.

'Just so you understand,' Jay said evenly. He turned away and picked up the fishing-rod that was resting against the outer wall of the hut. 'I think I'll go down to the river for an hour. Fishing's meant to have a very calming effect on—on just about everything,' he finished, with a wry grin.

Once he had gone, Charlie tried to keep herself occupied by getting their evening meal ready. It was impossible to stop a lot of very strange thoughts from floating through her mind, though. And perhaps the strangest of them all was the notion that she really wouldn't have minded too much if Jay *had* got carried away.

That's nonsense, she told herself fiercely. Philip showed you only too well what making love was really like. It's disgusting, it's painful, it's completely humiliating...

But perhaps it didn't have to be like that. Charlie stood very still as that possibility burst inside her head like a bombshell. And she was still standing there, going over and over that novel idea, when Jay came striding quickly back towards the hut.

Just the sight of him sent a taut quiver right through her, a curious mixture of excitement and unease. 'You've only been gone half an hour,' she said, nervousness making her voice come out much more sharply than she had intended. 'Dinner won't be ready for ages yet.'

Jay's brows were drawn together in a dark frown. 'I've been bitten by a snake,' he said briefly.

'What?' Everything else instantly forgotten, Charlie rushed over to him in sheer panic. 'What should I do? Do you feel ill, are you going to collapse?' Her eyes became absolutely huge with sudden fear. 'You're not going to die, are you?'

'It's highly unlikely, since the snake wasn't even poisonous,' Jay answered drily.

Charlie felt her knees sag as relief rushed over her. Then she rounded on him indignantly. 'Then why are you making all this fuss? Getting me worked up and scared to death over nothing?'

'You're the one who's turning it into a drama,' Jay pointed out with infuriating calmness. 'I merely said I'd been bitten by a snake. And I have.'

'Where?'

'On the ankle.'

Charlie looked down, then bit her lip with renewed anxiety as she saw the red, rather swollen patch of skin just above his shin-bone. 'How did it happen?' she asked.

'It was my own fault,' Jay replied irritably. 'I hadn't managed to catch a single fish, so I decided to try further downriver. There was a patch of long grass, and instead of going round it I walked straight through it. The snake must have been curled up in the middle of it, sun-bathing. I trod on its tail. Not surprisingly, it didn't take it too well, and it turned round and bit me.'

'You should have been more careful where you were putting your feet,' Charlie told him, without a great deal of sympathy. 'You're always lecturing me about keeping my eyes open.'

'Perhaps I had something else on my mind,' Jay growled. Charlie felt a flush of hot colour sweep over her face, then she looked away from him rather awkwardly.

'Does it hurt?' she mumbled a few moments later.

'It's not exactly painless. I'm not worried about that, though. What does bother me is that it could easily get infected. I suppose I'd better have a shot of penicillin, just as a precautionary measure.'

'When I was bitten by that ant, all I got was a dab of antiseptic cream,' she reminded him with a touch of acerbity.

'A snake bite's rather more serious than an ant bite,' came his immediate retort. 'And we can't afford to take chances in this sort of situation.' He got heavily to his feet. 'I'll get the penicillin, and a hypodermic.'

'It's all right, I'll fetch them,' Charlie said quickly. 'You'd better sit there and rest.' It didn't take her long to rummage through their comprehensive medical kit, and find what she needed. In a few minutes, she had rejoined Jay. 'I'll give you the injection, if you like,' she offered helpfully.

Jay's eyebrows instantly shot up. 'You'll do what?'

'Give you the injection,' she repeated patiently. 'It's a bit difficult to inject yourself—and a bit hair-raising!' she laughed.

'Thanks, but I don't fancy being stabbed by some amateur,' he growled darkly, and with a total lack of gratitude.

'Oh, I know all about giving injections,' Charlie assured him confidently. 'I had a friend at school who was a diabetic. She had to give herself regular shots of insulin, and I used to give her a hand when she got really fed up with doing it herself.' She expertly filled the hypodermic with the required amount of penicillin. 'Where would you like it?' she asked slyly.

Jay glared back at her. 'In my arm!'

He rolled up his shirtsleeve, and Charlie brandished the needle with a flourish. She was rather beginning to enjoy this. For the first time since meeting Jay Challoner, she was the one in charge of the situation, and it was definitely a good feeling. Then she glanced at his face, and her expression abruptly changed.

'You've gone as white as a sheet,' she said worriedly. 'Are you getting some sort of reaction to the bite? Are you *sure* that snake wasn't poisonous?'

'Absolutely certain. Just get on with the injection!'

He had gone even paler now; Charlie would never have believed anyone so tanned could lose so much colour. Then another possible reason for his pallor slowly dawned on her. She thought about it, but then shook her head because she was sure she had to be wrong. Then she took a closer look at Jay's face. There was a light beading of sweat on his skin, and the muscles around the base of his neck were absolutely rigid with tension. It looked as if her guess had been the right one!

'You're scared of injections,' she said slowly, but with a growing sense of glee. 'A great big man like you—and you're frightened to death of this tiny little needle!'

Jay shot her a baleful glance. 'Are you going to stand there and gloat, or are you going to give me this shot?'

Charlie grinned. 'I'll do it right now. And don't worry, it won't hurt—at least, not very much,' she added with bright cheerfulness.

A few seconds later, it was all over. The colour slowly returned to Jay's face, and he got to his feet. 'I'm going to lie down for a while,' he muttered. 'I don't want anything to eat.'

'Do you think you'll need another injection later?' Charlie enquired with deliberate wide-eyed innocence.

Jay glared back at her even more darkly. 'You really enjoyed that,' he accused.

'Yes, I did,' she admitted frankly. 'It's nice to discover you're human, that you've got a few weaknesses, just like the rest of us.'

For just an instant, his face changed. The heavy frown lifted, and something glittered brightly in the depths of his eyes. 'I've definitely got a couple of weak spots,' he assured her, in a voice that was suddenly much huskier than it had been a few moments ago. 'And if I didn't feel so damned bad, we could have a lot of fun finding out exactly what—and where—they are. All I want to do right now, though, is sleep. See you in the morning, Charlotte.' And, with that, he turned round and went into the hut, leaving her staring after him with a touch of her old edginess.

Before she climbed into her own hammock that evening, Charlie cautiously peered round the blanket that curtained off Jay's sleeping area. By the light of the candle she was holding, she could see his eyes were open and rather feverishly bright, and his skin was beaded with sweat.

'What's wrong?' she asked in some alarm.

'Nothing,' he got out through teeth that were chattering noisily. 'It's the penicillin—sometimes I get an allergic reaction to it. Don't worry, it only lasts a few hours. I'll sleep it off and be fine by the morning.'

'Is there anything you want? Anything I can do?'

He managed a faint grin. 'Under normal circumstances, the answer to both those questions would be "yes". Unfortunately, I don't feel up to it right now, so just go away and leave me alone with my fantasies, Charlotte.'

Flushing furiously, she pulled the blanket back into place. Then she undressed, pulled on her thin cotton nightie, and clambered into her own hammock. Obviously he wasn't feeling *that* ill; there was no need for her to lie awake all night worrying about him.

All the same, she didn't sleep very well. Around dawn, she woke up from yet another light, restless doze, and knew that this time there was no chance of her getting back to sleep again. She ran her fingers tiredly through the tangled skeins of her hair, then decided she had better check on Jay.

It always felt chilly this early in the morning. Shivering a little, she padded over to his section of the hut. She pulled back the dividing blanket, then found herself staring straight into one blue and one green eye.

'You're awake,' she said, rather unnecessarily.

'It rather looks like it,' he agreed.

'How do you feel?'

'Weak. But I think I'll live.' His gaze raked over her. 'You look frozen. Why don't you climb in with me and warm up?'

Charlie instantly stiffened. 'I don't think that's a very good idea.'

'Why not?' asked Jay comfortably. 'Sharing a hammock can be fun.'

'You're speaking from experience, of course,' she commented caustically.

He merely grinned and slid the cover of the sleeping-bag back invitingly. 'Come on, Charlotte, you've come a long way these last few days. Let's try and take it a little further.'

'Why?'

Her blunt question made the corners of his mouth twist into a quizzical line. After a moment, though, he answered her in a perfectly serious tone of voice. 'Because I think it would be a good thing for you to learn that it can be very pleasant, sharing a bed with a man. It's warm, it's companionable, it's nice to feel someone curled up next to you. And this would be a particularly good time for you to try sharing my bed. I don't feel as lousy as I did last night, but I've still got hardly enough energy to twitch my little finger. We won't run into any problems we can't handle. We can just lie here and enjoy being close.'

'I still don't think I want to do this,' Charlie told him. Yet there was far less conviction in her voice now, and she was a little alarmed to find she had actually taken a step towards the hammock.

'Don't be a coward,' Jay challenged softly. 'Take that next step, Charlotte. And the next. Start walking back into life again.'

Without quite knowing how it had happened, she found herself standing beside him.

'Careful how you get in,' he warned drily, 'or you'll tip us both on to the floor.'

She climbed in very gingerly, still telling herself that this was probably the craziest thing she had ever done in her life. She eased herself down inside the sleeping-bag, then waited tensely to see if her body was going to play any of its old tricks on her, swamping her with wave after wave of utter revulsion at this physical closeness to a male body.

To her astonishment, though, nothing happened. At least, nothing unpleasant. Instead, she felt the hard warmth of Jay's body curled against her back, and it seemed strange for a while, but it was amazing how soon she grew used to it. He was obviously very relaxed and at ease; she got the impression he was already half asleep. But why shouldn't he be relaxed? she asked herself with an unexpected pang of resentment. He'd probably lain like this a hundred times before. Not with her, of course, but with a whole string of gorgeous women, all of whom had been more than willing to be coaxed into his bed.

Then Charlie was devastated by a strong wave of jealousy that rolled over her without the slightest warning. When it had finally gone, she blinked in disbelief. Why on earth had that happened? It was a crazy way to react, she told herself shakily. No one could get that jealous, unless...

Unless what? She gave a quick, deep shiver, and decided that she definitely didn't want to answer that question.

'Still cold?' murmured Jay sleepily, obviously feeling the brief shudder that had run through her. 'Curl up a bit closer.'

She was lying with her back to him, and she could feel his warm breath gently brushing the nape of her neck. He shifted position slightly, easing himself still nearer, until the powerful male length of him was in contact with her from head to toe. And he had been right, Charlie told herself with new haziness. This was the sort of experience no one should miss out on. It was like floating in a sea of warmth and love.

Her nerves gave another sharp and unexpected twitch. There it was—that word again, the same word she had tried so very hard to avoid earlier. She firmly pushed it to the very back of her mind, where it could be safely locked away and ignored. Things were complicated enough already without bringing that sort of entanglement into it.

Jay gave a grunt of satisfaction, then experimentally ran a finger down the line of her spine. 'How do you feel about all this so far?' he asked lazily.

Charlie decided it would be far safer not to tell him. Instead, she tried to edge away from him a little. 'I don't think I like it very much,' she said stiffly.

Jay merely chuckled. 'Liar! But it's fine by me if you want to pretend you're not enjoying every minute of this.'

'You're so big-headed!' she muttered. 'I suppose you think it's every woman's idea of heaven, to sleep in your bed.'

'Not many of them want to sleep,' he told her, with an even deeper laugh.

Pure indignation washed over her. This man was quite impossible! She turned over, ready to confront him, then somehow found herself wedged right up against him. An instant later, her eyes flew wide open. Locked together like this, it was impossible not to be aware that he had instantly responded to the warm closeness of her body.

'Don't panic,' came his calm instruction, no trace of apology or embarrassment in his voice. 'I suppose it was bound to happen. It needn't go any further—if you don't want it to.'

Charlie's heart began to hammer wildly. 'You were faking it earlier,' she accused. 'Telling me that you hardly had enough energy to move!'

'Half faking it,' Jay conceded. 'I really did feel rough when I first woke up. Things seem to have improved rather dramatically in the last few minutes, though,' he went on in a voice that had suddenly grown low and husky.

Charlie started to struggle free of him, but somehow that only made matters worse. Her breasts were brushing against his chest now, and that seemed to trigger off a whole new load of sensations. It felt as if someone was setting off a dazzling firework display somewhere deep inside her. And the sparks seemed to be spraying all over her, igniting equally disturbing fires in her highly sensitive nerve-ends.

Rather belatedly, she realised Jay wasn't making the slightest attempt to hold on to her. He was just lying there, studying her with those extraordinary eyes of his and letting their bright gaze silently tell her that the decision was entirely hers. She could go or stay, as she pleased.

And she was staggered by how difficult that decision was. For several long moments, she actually wavered; it seemed incredibly hard to move. Then common sense took over. She gave a great gasp, half fell out of the hammock, and then dashed wildly out of the hut.

Outside, the early morning sun filtered through the trees, splashing everything with its pale light, while the different sounds echoed from the forest—some melodic, some harsh. The air was still pleasantly cool. It soon drained the heat from her hot skin, and her breathing slowly returned to normal.

She stood there for ages, not even realising where she was. All her thoughts, her tangled emotions, were focused on something deep within her. And all she could hear was a voice inside her head telling her that this could be the most important decision she would ever make.

In the end, she didn't really make the final decision at all. Some inborn instinct seemed to take over and guide her. For a few minutes, she lifted her face, feeling the sunlight washing over her skin like a warm, healing balm. Then she turned round and slowly, steadily, walked back into the hut.

CHAPTER EIGHT

JAY was no longer lying in the hammock. Instead, he was dressing, pulling on a shirt as Charlie walked over to him.

He didn't say a word; he just looked at her steadily, his eyes darkening a fraction as they studied her face.

'You always seem to know what I'm thinking,' she said in a low voice. 'Do you know what's going on inside my head right now?'

'It's not hard to work out,' Jay said slowly. 'But are you sure?'

She gave a slightly helpless shrug. 'I don't know what it's like to feel sure about something like this. But I came back,' she reminded him unevenly.

'So you did.' He hesitated a moment longer, then his fingers curled round her wrist and gently but firmly pulled her closer. 'But understand this, Charlotte,' he went on a little thickly. 'I'm not superhuman, I've got limits like everyone else. If you want to change your mind again, don't leave it too late. Once I get past a certain point, there might be no turning back.'

'I think—I think it'll be all right,' she whispered shakily.

His mouth curled into a faint smile. 'Just relax, don't get too worked up about it,' he advised gently. 'It's not some sort of exam. You won't get a pass or fail mark at the end of it.'

'I don't want to—disappoint you,' Charlie blurted out.

'You've not disappointed me for a minute since the moment we first met,' he told her. 'In fact, this whole trip's turned out to be a fairly memorable experience,' he added drily.

'But——'

'Stop talking,' Jay instructed. 'I don't go for long conversations in bed. Just tell me what you like—or what you don't like——'

His fingers had left her wrist now. Instead, they were trailing lightly down her spine, exploring the delicate outline of the bone and the contrasting softness of the hollows in between.

'I like that,' she told him shyly.

'You'll like it even better without clothes on,' came his relaxed response. Even before he had finished speaking, his fingers had expertly started to peel off her thin cotton nightie. Charlie stiffened slightly as she stood there in just her brief pants, but there wasn't really time to feel awkward. Jay had already drawn her close again and, as his own shirt swung open, she felt the hard tips of her breasts graze against his skin. Deliberately, he increased the delicious tactile contact, gently crushing her softness against him, then releasing her again so he could explore the full swell, the aching peaks, with the warm palm of his hand. Familiar, joyous sensations began to shoot through her, and she sagged against him as her legs went weak. His hands instantly slid round to the satin-smooth hollow of her back, more than willing to provide the support she needed. Then his fingers stayed there for a long while, sometimes resting against her gently quivering skin, sometimes moving restlessly, wandering randomly in all directions, rubbing lightly against the line of her hip and the swell of her buttocks, before returning to rest comfortably against the base of her spine.

She responded to his touch with small, involuntary shivers of pleasure. Her breasts were crushed harder against him now, and a moment later he bent his head, locking his mouth against hers in a deep, exploratory kiss that went on and on until she was dizzy and disorientated.

When Jay finally lifted his head again, his eyes were dark and glittering, and she could feel the fast, hard pounding of his heart.

'So far, so good,' he said a little unsteadily. 'Have I done anything yet you don't like?'

Charlie shook her head. She didn't trust herself to speak. She was sure her voice would only come out as a feeble squeak.

'Good,' murmured Jay, with some satisfaction. 'Then let's get to know each other even better.'

His hands curled more tightly around the small of her back. Then he drew her even closer, so she fitted snugly against him, curve locked to hollow, hips and thighs coming together like two matching pieces of a jigsaw, warm skin clamped against warm skin, so that Charlie suddenly found it hard to figure out where her own body ended and Jay's began. It was such an incredible experience, being this close to a vibrantly aroused male without feeling sick and disgusted, that she just revelled in it for a while. She seemed to be floating in a sort of limbo where everything was suddenly, miraculously, all right, and would stay all right because she knew she could trust this man completely. He would never hurt her, force her into humiliating and painful positions, frantically use her to try and arouse a response from his inadequate body.

With willing eagerness, she let him rock her rhythmically against him, the gentle friction having an instant effect on him. His hard maleness pressed into her own soft flesh with new forcefulness, while his arms held her prisoner so she couldn't draw away from him.

'I want you to get used to the touch of me, the feel of me,' he told her huskily. 'I don't want you ever to be frightened of a single part of me.'

'I'm not frightened of you,' she whispered with a sense of wonder.

'And do you like this?' he prompted softly, burrowing still closer, so that she had the whirling impression that they were already joined together, that the thin, frustrating barrier of light cotton had somehow magically dissolved.

'I love it,' she answered simply. 'I love being touched by you, wanted by you.' She didn't even think what she was saying. 'Jay, I love——'

Charlie stopped abruptly, shaken to the roots by what she had so nearly blurted out. Oh God, did he know what she had been going to say to him? She was sure that he did. Although they were still locked very close, their bodies welded together like some living, erotic sculpture, he had somehow withdrawn from her just a fraction. The magical harmony wasn't there any longer, it was as if he had just retreated behind a closed door. And she realised almost straight away that she didn't like that. It was almost harder to bear than his physical withdrawal, which came just a few moments later.

Neither of them said anything for several long, tense seconds. In the end, it was Charlie who couldn't bear the silence any longer, who muttered the first thing that came into her head.

'What is it? What's the matter?'

But she didn't really need him to answer; she knew very well what the matter was. She had almost said something that neither of them had expected to hear. And, from Jay's immediate reaction, it was fairly obvious that her blurted confession had had a devastating effect on him.

Jay took another step back from her, and when she found the nerve to look at him, she saw his features were shadowed with a mixture of frustration and something which she had never expected to see there—self-disgust. It was clear that there was a fierce conflict suddenly raging inside him; a conflict which he hadn't expected, didn't want, and didn't know how to handle.

A few moments later, he swung right away from her, his entire body tense.

'Charlotte, I think it would be a good idea if you got out of here for a while,' he growled.

'You—you don't want me to stay?' she stammered.

His gaze flicked over her, and she flinched as she saw the new storminess in his eyes. 'Yes, I want you to stay. All I'm aching to do right now is to toss you straight into that hammock and keep you there until I'm too exhausted to move. But I don't think that would turn out too well for either of us, not at this particular moment. That's why you'd better get away from me. And stay away—or you might not like the consequences.'

It was the grim, dark expression on his face that convinced her she had better do exactly as he had instructed. Grabbing hold of her nightdress, which had been discarded so joyously only minutes ago, she fled blindly out of the hut. Then she sat outside with her knees curled up tightly to her chin, shivering despite the heat.

How could it suddenly have all gone so wrong? And what on earth had made her so very nearly tell him that she loved him?

Because it was the truth? whispered a small voice inside her head. Charlie instantly closed her mind to that possibility. It wasn't true—it *couldn't* be true. Although she had come a long way these last couple of weeks, she definitely wasn't ready to fall in love. She might never feel capable of coping with a major emotional upheaval like that.

It was over an hour before Jay finally left the hut and walked over to join her.

'You'd better get dressed,' he told her quietly. 'We need to talk, and that nightdress is—just a little too distracting,' he finished drily.

She didn't argue with him. She simply went into the hut, pulled on shorts and a cotton shirt, and then went back to stand a safe distance away from him.

'What happened was entirely my fault,' Jay began without any preamble. 'I chose one hell of a time to realise I had no right to take you to bed. It's something I never even thought about before, the moral rights and wrongs of what I was doing. Fortunately, I came to my senses before things finally went too far—even though I did leave it until the very last minute.'

'But I thought it was what you—what you wanted,' Charlie muttered hesitantly.

'It was. It still is,' Jay confirmed, with a slightly grim twist of his mouth. 'But that doesn't make it right.' His gaze became a little more intense. 'Do you know what I've been doing these past couple of weeks? Playing God,' he said with some disgust. 'Setting myself up as the one person who could put your life straight again, make you realise you could cope with—even enjoy—a relationship with a man.'

'But you succeeded,' she reminded him shakily. 'You really did put things right for me.'

'Did that give me the right to reap the rewards?' he queried sharply. 'And what the hell made me think I even had the right to interfere in the first place? Then there's the million-dollar-question—where does it finally end, Charlotte? At what point do I say, OK, you're cured, so off you go and face the world on your own?'

She shook her head miserably. 'I don't know.'

'Neither do I,' he said roughly. 'So that's why this thing's got to finish right now, before I do you any real harm.'

At that, her head shot up. 'Harm?' she echoed incredulously. 'How on earth can it have harmed me to learn that it can feel good to touch a man? Even better to have him touch me?'

'The harm comes when you realise that's *all* I'm offering, that there's nothing else,' Jay replied quietly.

So she had been right, she told herself numbly. It was that half-blurted-out confession of love that had made him draw back so suddenly, causing this abrupt and painful rift between them. He had suddenly realised he was getting involved in far more than he had bargained for.

'I want you to get several very important things straight in your head,' Jay went on steadily. 'It's difficult to keep things in perspective in a place like this,' he said, staring at the lush green forest that encircled them. 'Everything seems to take on a slightly fairy-tale aspect after a while. I'm not some make-believe prince, though. I've not worked any magic and I'm not going to whisk you off to a city of gold where we'll both live happily ever after. I've just taught you to enjoy physical contact, that's all. Any man with enough time and patience could have done the same. You were ready to learn. All I had to do was break down those last few barriers you were hanging on to.'

'I don't think you should underestimate what you've done,' she told him in a low voice.

She saw the first glint of temper show in his eyes. 'My God, you're still looking at me as if I'm some kind of miracle worker,' he said forcefully. 'I'm not! Why won't you understand that? I'm just a normal man, with the usual male weaknesses.' He glared at her fiercely. 'Do

you want to hear the real reason why I brought you with
me to Ecuador?'

'Because you needed a secretary,' whispered Charlie,
shrinking back a little from that sudden blaze of anger.

'And do you really think I couldn't have found
someone suitable, once I'd arrived in this country?'

'But you said——'

'I said what suited me at the time,' Jay cut in tersely.
'But perhaps this is a good moment for you to hear a
few truths—although I don't think you're going to like
them very much. You want to know why I brought you
with me? It's because you're a blonde,' he said bluntly.
'And blondes turn me on.' Ignoring her sharp gasp, he
went on. 'From the day I first saw you, when you came
to the hotel for that interview, I knew I wanted to get
involved with you. Do you know what first attracts one
person to another?' he questioned her harshly. 'It's their
physical appearance. Other things might come into it
later, but that's what initially hooks their interest. I've
always gone for blondes, and you were the most gorgeous one I'd seen for a long time. I gave you the job
because I was determined to keep you around. I thought
that, with luck, the attraction might turn out to be
mutual.'

Charlie stared at him in shock. 'I—I don't believe
that,' she said a little frantically.

Jay's mouth set into a grim line. 'You'd better believe
it. Remember when we talked about Philip? I told you
then that a man's sexual response is fixed quite early in
his life, that it hardly ever changes—and I'm no ex-
ception. My first serious affair was with a stunning
blonde. I didn't love her, but she certainly triggered off
something inside me. She was like a drug, I couldn't
keep away from her—she knew enough tricks in bed to
keep me totally hooked. Even when the affair was finally over, that trigger response still worked. I only had

to see a blonde, and I'd get the same physical reaction, a strong sexual response.' His gaze raked over her white face. 'Well?' he challenged tautly. 'What do you think of your Prince Charming now? Perhaps you're thinking that I'm really no better than Philip, it's just that we're turned on by different things. And maybe you're right to think that way.'

Confused and bewildered, Charlie couldn't get a single word out of her constricted throat.

'You don't like this little lecture on what makes the male animal tick?' enquired Jay, his voice uncharacteristically hard. 'Come to think of it, I'm not much enjoying giving it. A man likes to keep his weaknesses safely hidden away. Things were starting to get complicated, though, Charlotte. What started out as a game was beginning to turn into something else. I suddenly realised I had to put a stop to it before you got hurt.'

That stung a reaction out of her. 'And you think this isn't hurting me?' she flung back at him.

'Yes, it probably is,' he agreed grimly. 'But it's better to do it now, rather than leave it until later, when it'll cause far more damage.'

She stared at his dark, shadowed features. 'I feel as if I don't know you,' she said at last, with a small shiver. 'I thought I did—but I don't.'

'Yes, you do,' he contradicted her. 'I'm still the same person you've lived with these last couple of weeks. You're just seeing another side of me, that's all. A less likeable side,' he added with marked reluctance.

'You're right, I don't like it much,' Charlie muttered a few moments later. 'But I suppose you're trying to be truthful—even honourable——'

'Honourable?' Jay repeated caustically. 'Don't credit me with motives I haven't got. I'm trying to get out of a situation that I should never have got into in the first place. Do you think that's particularly honourable?'

'But when it came down to it you wouldn't make love to me. A lot of men would have—have just taken what they wanted,' she got out at last, rather painfully.

'I damned nearly did! God knows how I kept my hands off you.' He paused briefly, then went on more quietly. 'Right from the very start, I knew I wanted to have an affair with you. It's why I hired you, why I brought you here to Ecuador. I thought that working together would be the best way of eventually building up a closer relationship.' Jay shrugged. 'It was a gamble, of course. We might have hated one another once we started spending a lot of time together. But I decided it was worth the risk. You interested me more than any woman I'd known in a very long time.'

Charlie gave a slightly bitter laugh. 'You must have got quite a shock when you found what you'd actually taken on—someone who couldn't even stand to be touched.'

'It was a shock,' he agreed. 'And when I found out *why*, I was angry. Very, very angry. No one's got the right to ruin someone's life the way Philip ruined yours. So I gave up any plans I'd had for a casual, pleasant affair, and decided I'd try to put things right for you.' His mouth twisted into a fierce, hard line. 'How arrogant can you get? I thought I could interfere in your life, straighten out all your hang-ups for you, and not once—*not once*—did I ever stop and think about the consequences, consider the full implications of what I was doing. It wasn't until I saw you looking at me with that trusting, loving look in your eyes that something exploded inside my head. I finally realised what I'd done. I'd set myself up as some kind of superhero in your eyes, I was making you totally dependent on me. Where was it supposed to end, though? And, more important than that, what was meant to happen after we'd made love, and the whole thing had been wildly and gloriously successful? Did I get up, pronounce you "cured", and then just walk away from you?'

'You're assuming that it *would* have been successful,' Charlie flashed, with a first touch of resentment.

His gaze locked on to hers and easily held it. 'Do you think it wouldn't have been?' he challenged.

She didn't want to answer that. Instead, she dragged her eyes away from his and stared down at the ground. 'There's an alternative to this mess we're in now,' she muttered, finding it a little hard to get the words out, because her heart had started to beat uncomfortably fast. 'Why shouldn't we just stick to your first plan? Have an affair that we'll both—both enjoy?' She stumbled over that last part, but determinedly finished it.

Instantly, and without even thinking about it, Jay shook his head. 'It wouldn't work, Charlotte. When we first met, you fooled me with that gorgeous blonde hair and those inviting blue eyes. I thought you knew the score, that you weren't getting into anything you couldn't handle. I know you so much better now, though. You're just not equipped to cope with that sort of situation. You're too much of an innocent.'

'Innocent!' she echoed in disbelief. 'After those six months of hell with Philip?'

'Innocence is a state of mind. It's got nothing to do with physical experience. You're not cut out for casual affairs, and you never will be.' Jay shrugged regretfully. 'I wish I could offer you more, but I can't. My own life's pretty unsettled right now, and I'm not looking for any further complications. Once I've finished the lecture tour in America, I don't know which way my career will be going. If my novel turns out well, I might stick to writing fiction for a while. Alternatively, I might eventually go back to serious anthropology. Contrary to what you probably think, I'm not a playboy by nature. I enjoy getting involved with serious research. The only thing

I'm certain about is that I'm not looking for a serious, settled relationship. It's not the right time in my life for such a commitment. I don't *want* it.'

'And I don't get any say in the matter?'

'No, you don't,' he confirmed, with utter finality. His features softened a fraction. 'You think this isn't hard for me?' he added more sombrely. 'Do you think I wouldn't give my right hand to take what you're offering? But it wouldn't be any good, Charlotte. You'd end up badly hurt, I'd feel damned guilty, and the whole thing would turn into the sort of emotional mess that we can both well do without. That's why it's much better to put an end to it right now, and each get on with our own lives.'

She knew how completely useless it would be to argue with him. He wasn't a man who would ever change his mind once it was firmly made up. Anyway, she wasn't sure she was capable of any rational arguments at the moment. He was right, seeing this new side of him had left her in a state of shock. She had got used to the relaxed, easy-going man she had known these last couple of weeks. Why hadn't she ever suspected these darker motives and emotions were hidden just below the surface?

Probably because she hadn't *wanted* to know, she told herself tiredly. Love was definitely blind, and rather late in the day she was forced to admit that love was what she felt for Jay Challoner. Love, desire, a mental bond and a physical need—and perhaps, even after all he had said, a touch of hero-worship that wouldn't quite die, that all his blunt words couldn't quite wipe out.

But he had just made it perfectly clear that he wasn't interested in her new-found adoration. Perhaps because of his unorthodox life-style, he was a man used to casual affairs, where neither side demanded too much of the other. It was a pattern that obviously suited him, and he clearly had no desire to change it.

He had turned away from her now, and Charlie took the hint; she got up and slowly walked back to the hut. Heavy clouds were drifting across the sky, cutting off the bright sunshine and plunging the clearing into heavy shadow, but she didn't care. It suited her dark, introspective mood. In the space of just an hour, her world had started to crumble around her for the second time in her life. Rather desperately, she wondered if she was capable of picking up the pieces and sticking them back together yet again.

The next couple of days definitely weren't easy. Jay didn't seem able to shake off a black moodiness, which Charlie suspected was foreign to him. She also had the feeling that he deeply resented the fact that she was drawing out this darker side of his nature. Occasionally, she would turn round to find his gaze fixed on her with fierce intensity. He would instantly look away again, though, and sometimes even got up and strode off, as if he found any sort of contact with her difficult. The easy camaraderie of the last couple of weeks, when they had been relaxed and comfortable in each other's company, had vanished without a trace. In its place was an edgy truce which threatened to fall apart at any moment, and without warning.

On the third morning, Charlie didn't clamber out of her hammock until quite late. It wasn't that she was tired—far from it. Most of the time, she was filled with a restless energy that kept her prowling around during the day and tossing sleeplessly for much of the night. It was just that she didn't want to have to face Jay any sooner than was absolutely necessary. The atmosphere between them was so tense at times that she half expected to see small puffs of smoke hanging in the air after he had shot yet another of those smouldering glances at her!

When she finally made her way out into the main section of the hut, she found Jay was sitting at the table, going through the folders which held the neatly typed opening chapters of his novel. Neither of them had made any effort to get any work done during the last couple of days. Now, though, she looked at the folders warily. Had he decided he wanted to get back to work? Oh God, she hoped not! The thought of having to sit close to him and take dictation, to listen to the dark velvet sound of his voice, made her go physically cold. The situation was tense enough as it was. Surely he wasn't going to go out of his way to make things even worse?

Then he glanced up at her and, when she saw the cold expression in those odd-coloured eyes of his, a warning bell began to clang loudly inside her head. He was angry about something. No, not just angry—downright furious!

Jay put one of the folders down on the table, then studied her with that freezing look again. Something began to shrivel up inside Charlie, and she wondered what on earth she had done to make him stare at her like that.

'I always knew you were a clever girl, Charlotte,' he said at last, in a voice that sounded tired and yet totally contemptuous. 'But I'm only just beginning to appreciate *how* clever.'

She licked lips that had suddenly gone very dry. 'What—what do you mean?'

Jay's gaze became even more icy. 'When I first interviewed you back in London, you told me you worked free-lance, as a temporary secretary. So how come you've got a folder full of notes about me? Notes which are obviously going to be used as the basis for a magazine or newspaper article?'

Charlie felt her stomach begin to churn. He had found the rough drafts of her feature story! The story which she hadn't even thought about for the last few days, and which she now knew she would never write.

'How did you find that folder?' she got out jerkily at last. 'I thought I'd——'

'You thought you'd hidden it where I'd never see it?' he finished for her in a grim tone. 'Yes, you did. It was just unlucky for you that I couldn't find some notes I made a couple of days ago. I turned the hut upside down looking for them—and found this instead.' His eyes bored right into her. 'Who do you really work for, Charlotte?'

'*Tomorrow* magazine,' she admitted dully. She sat down rather heavily on one of the small camp stools, and twisted her fingers together with a restless unhappiness. 'I suppose you're not interested in hearing an explanation?' she muttered, although without much hope.

'Too damned right, I'm not!' Jay got to his feet, his eyes abruptly ablaze with pure contempt. 'You told me once you were a convincing liar, and I should have believed you. I've certainly swallowed every lie you've told me since the day we first met—and there must have been quite a few of them,' he added in disgust. 'You're a good secretary, Charlotte. But my guess is that you're an even better journalist. You certainly must have had a lot of practice at this sort of thing, to have pulled it off so slickly, so cleverly. Is this how you usually get your stories?' he enquired with caustic anger. 'By using every underhanded trick you can think of to worm your way into someone else's life and confidence?'

Charlie opened her mouth, ready to defend herself. Who was he, to accuse her of being underhanded? On his own admission, he had only given her the job as his secretary because he had wanted to have an affair with her!

But then her indignation died away as swiftly as it had surged over her. It wasn't the same thing at all, no matter which way she looked at it. When things had started to get too serious between them, he had been completely— almost brutally—truthful with her, even though it had been to his own detriment. She had had no plans for being equally honest with him in return, though. He was right. Her behaviour had been totally despicable. Looking back, she couldn't quite believe she had done all the things she had; lying to him quite cheerfully so she could get that job as his temporary secretary, and then keeping up the pretence so she could dig around and try to get the material she needed for her story.

She supposed it would have been easy to have blamed it all on Dan Marshall, her editor; to have convinced herself that he had more or less forced her into it, and not given her any choice—except, possibly, the sack! But she knew it hadn't really been like that. She had gone into the whole thing willingly enough. The only thing that had bothered her was the possibility that Jay might see through her cover story, ruining her chance of getting enough information for the feature.

Now that she was forced to face the truth head on, she was completely appalled at the way she had behaved. During the last few days, her sense of right and wrong seemed to have somehow clicked back into place. Given a similar choice right now, she knew she would rather lose her job than go about getting a story in such an unscrupulous way. It was too late to try and explain all that to Jay, though. He didn't want to hear any excuses, any apologies. In fact, right now he looked as if he would like to wring her neck!

Jay came a little closer, and she flinched as she saw his face had become even more grim, and darkly threatening. 'Just how much of it was lies?' he demanded hoarsely. 'Some of it, most of it—*all* of it? That tale you spun me about your marriage and the hell you went through—was that something you made up as well? Did you think it would lend extra spice to your story? Were you going to include it in your article, add a little bit of titillation to grab the attention of your readers?'

Charlie went completely white. For a few moments, she couldn't believe he had actually made such a disgusting accusation.

'Believe whatever you like!' she flung back at him in a choked voice. Then she couldn't stop herself adding bitterly, 'I suppose you think I carved those initials on my own chest, just to make the whole thing authentic!'

This time, Jay was the one who lost a lot of colour. 'No, I don't think that,' he muttered tautly, at last. 'But, my God, Charlotte, I can't sort the truth from the lies right now. And I'm not sure I even want to try—I don't know that you're worth the effort.'

She stared at him through eyes that were so blurred that they could only just see the anger and bleak disillusionment that had shadowed his features. In another moment, she knew she would go down on her knees and *beg* him to give her a chance to try to explain how it had happened; how her disastrous marriage had warped her whole outlook on life, leaving her cynical and coldhearted, making her behave in a way quite foreign to her true nature.

While she was still struggling with her raw emotions, though, a familiar buzzing noise broke through all the confusion inside her head. She looked up dazedly and saw that Jay was also staring up at the sky. A moment later, his brows drew together in a dark frown.

'It's a plane,' he said tautly. 'Probably the one that brought us here.'

'But—it's not due for several more days,' Charlie muttered numbly.

'The pilot must have come back early, for some reason. It's definitely going to land,' he added, watching as the small plane circled round and lost height. 'I'd better go and meet it.'

He turned and quickly strode off, as if relieved to have a legitimate excuse to get away from her. After a few seconds, though, Charlie began to stumble after him. She knew he didn't want her with him, but she couldn't bear the thought of being on her own right now. She didn't think she could stand her own company.

In a couple of minutes, they had reached the landing-strip. The small plane had already landed safely and taxied to a halt. As they walked towards it, the pilot jumped out and gave them a cheerful grin.

'Glad to see you're all right. When there weren't any radio messages from you, we began to get worried. I finally decided I'd better fly in, to make sure you weren't in any sort of trouble.'

'The radio's dead,' Jay explained briefly. 'We couldn't make contact with anyone. Apart from that, there haven't been any major problems. I think we'd both like to get out of here, though. Can you fly us back with you? We could be ready to leave in about an hour.'

'No problem,' nodded the pilot. 'We'll take off as soon as you're ready.'

Charlie was listening to the conversation in numbed silence, and Jay's words at last sank in. They were getting out of here. She was going home!

She knew she ought to be feeling relieved, perhaps even elated. This crazy trip was finally over. In just an hour, she would be on her way back to civilisation and sanity. She could put the last couple of weeks behind her and get on with her life. And it was going to be a very different life from now on, she was already deter-

mined about that. Over the last few days—with Jay's
help—she had finally shaken herself free of the dark
legacy that had haunted her these past three years. And,
perhaps even more important than that, she had
somehow got back her sense of right and wrong. Too
late to do her any good where Jay was concerned, of
course, but at least she was utterly determined not to
lose it again in the future.

But what sort of future was it going to be? Dreary
and colourless, answered a suddenly joyless voice inside
her head. And why? Because she was going to have to
live without the man who had straightened everything
out for her; the man who had looked at her with such
cold disgust just minutes ago, as he had told her she
wasn't worth the effort of trying to understand why she
had lied to him. And he was certainly in no mood to
ever forgive her.

Charlie gave a small shudder. This place might look
like paradise, but right at this very moment it felt like
absolute hell. And she had the awful feeling that nothing
was really going to change once she was back in London,
because one fact stood out with painful clarity. No matter
where she lived, where she went, Jay Challoner wasn't
going to be there.

CHAPTER NINE

CHARLIE stared at the walls of her small bedsitter, and dully wondered why she had never found them so deadly claustrophobic before. Sometimes they actually seemed to be closing in on her. She had to stifle the impulse to rush over and try to push them back again.

She supposed it was because she had got so used to spending hours in the open air during the last couple of weeks. It was funny, but while she had been in South America she had spent much of her time eagerly looking forward to getting back to civilisation again. Now she was here, though, London often seemed crowded and unbearably noisy. There were times when she positively ached for the peace and the solitude of the forest.

She and Jay had parted in South America with hardly more than a few polite words to each other. He had booked her on the first available flight back home, but had stayed behind himself, although she didn't know for how long. She knew he planned to go and see Jim Fielding in the hospital, to tell him that the trip had been a wash-out, and that he hadn't been able to carry on with Jim's research project. She had no idea where he would go after that, or what he planned to do—and she hadn't felt she had the right to ask him.

So here she was, back in London, with her life in a total mess for the second time around. And it was even worse than she had thought it would be. Inside her, there seemed to be a permanent knot of pain that got a little bigger, a little more unmanageable, with every day that passed. She knew perfectly well what was causing it; the only trouble was, she didn't have the slightest idea what to do about it.

If she had had plenty of work to have got on with, that might have made the situation slightly more bearable. Dan hadn't been pleased, though, when she had come back from South America without a story. In fact, to say that he hadn't taken it well was most definitely an understatement! She could still see his furious face as she had stood in front of his desk and told him there wasn't going to be any article on Jay Challoner.

'What is this, Charlie?' he had roared. 'Some sort of joke?'

'No joke,' she had told him resolutely. 'I can't do the story, and that's that. I'm sorry, but——'

'Sorry?' he had interrupted, his brows drawing together ominously. '*Sorry?* You're away from the office for damned near a month, and you come back with nothing? And don't tell me you couldn't get enough material for that feature. Only a half-wit could have spent all that time with Jay Challoner, and not dug up all the information they needed. You're definitely not stupid, Charlie, so what's this all about?'

But she had stubbornly refused to go into any details. 'I just can't do the feature, that's all.'

His face had darkened still further. 'That is definitely not all! I can't afford to carry people who don't pull their weight. This magazine operates on a tight budget, you know that as well as I do. What would happen if everyone strolled in and announced they couldn't come up with the story they'd been working on? You've done some good work for me, Charlie, but I might have to think twice about keeping you on if you're going to keep pulling this sort of stunt. Perhaps you'd better take the rest of the day off, to think things over. Come and see me again tomorrow. Maybe by then we'll both be in a more—reasonable frame of mind,' he had finished meaningfully.

But Charlie hadn't gone back. Instead, she had rung him later that afternoon and told him she wanted to resign.

Dan was in a much calmer mood by then. He spent quite some time trying to talk her out of it; he even rather grudgingly apologised for losing his temper that morning. Charlie hadn't changed her mind, though. She knew the same sort of situation was bound to come up at some time in the future. Dan would want her to use some underhanded method to get a story, and she was well aware that her new-found scruples wouldn't let her. She would have to refuse, and then this row would just start up all over again. It was best to get out now, to make a completely clean break. In the end, Dan was forced to accept her resignation. Charlie finally put down the phone, and then rather shakily began to wonder what on earth she was going to do with her life now.

Before she could begin to concentrate on the future, though, she knew there were several things connected with the nightmare of her past that still had to be dealt with. She wasn't looking forward to them, but she was grimly determined not to back out now. She had made a silent promise to herself to put her life in order, and that was exactly what she intended to do.

A couple of days later, she made an appointment to see a specialist. He was both helpful and sympathetic. Yes, he told her, he could definitely do something about the scars on her chest. It would be a fairly lengthy and expensive business, but at the end of it the scars should be virtually invisible. How soon could he begin treating her? Next week, if that suited her.

That suited her very well. The expense would be no problem, either. Charlie had already decided she would

pay for it out of the money Philip had left her. It would
be the first and last time she would ever touch it. She
would use it to pay for the damage he had inflicted on
her, then never draw out another penny. She had no
qualms about using it for such a purpose. It seemed only
right.

Next, she got in touch with the solicitors who were
dealing with Philip's estate. Initially, they were surprised—even a little shocked—when she told them she
wanted to turn over Ashborne Hall and its treasures to
an organisation such as the National Trust. Soon,
though, they were assuring her they would look into it
at once, to find out if such an arrangement was possible.
She had one further request to make of them. The competent voice on the other end of the phone told her it
would be dealt with immediately, and that there wouldn't
be any problems.

On Saturday morning, Charlie packed a small bag with
a change of clothes and a few personal items. She had
hardly slept at all the night before. She was absolutely
dreading the programme she had mapped out for herself
for the next couple of days, and told herself she was
crazy to voluntarily put herself through all this un-
necessary mental torment. Something inside her was
stubbornly insisting that it had to be done, though; that
she was never going to be quite free of the past unless
she forced herself to go through with this last—and most
difficult—of the plans she had made.

She phoned for a taxi to take her to the station; then
she sat, waiting for it, with her teeth already chattering
with nerves. When the doorbell rang, she actually
jumped several inches. Then she picked up her bag, drew
in a deep, unsteady breath, and walked slowly over to
the door.

When she opened it, all she was aware of at first was a tall, broad male figure that seemed to dominate the doorway. Recognition finally registered in her shocked brain, and she stared dazedly up into those all-too-familiar eyes: one blue and one green.

'You're not the taxi-driver,' she spluttered rather inanely.

'No, I'm not,' agreed Jay calmly. 'He won't be coming. I bumped into him on the doorstep and sent him away.'

'But you can't do that!' Charlie protested slightly wildly. 'I've got a train to catch, I'll miss it.'

'I'll drive you to the station. But we've got a few things to talk about first.'

'I thought you didn't want to talk to me ever again,' she retorted. 'Not to a totally disreputable journalist, who's written a revealing article about your private life.'

Jay looked at her steadily. 'I phoned your editor when I got back to England,' he said at last. 'I told him I'd sue if his magazine printed so much as a single word about me. And do you know what his reply was?'

As Charlie numbly shook her head, Jay leant comfortably back against the doorpost, looking infuriatingly relaxed. 'He said it was rather hard to publish an article that hadn't even been written. And that was never *going* to be written.'

'Oh,' said Charlie, a little shakenly. Then she stiffened as Jay levered himself upright and walked into the flat, decisively closing the door behind him. 'You've no right to barge in like this,' she complained, but somehow her voice didn't sound as indignant as she had intended. Just the sight of him seemed to drain away any resistance she might have been going to put up.

Jay glanced at her bag. 'Going away?'

'Just for a couple of days,' she answered, her tone suddenly guarded.

His eyes abruptly narrowed. 'Where to?'

'I really don't see that that's any of your business!' she snapped back, responding instinctively to the edge that had crept into his own voice.

He just kept looking at her in that steady, speculative way, until Charlie flushed and turned away from him.

'You're going to Ashborne Hall,' Jay stated evenly, a few moments later.

Charlie whirled back and glared at him. 'How many times have I told you to stop poking around inside my head? It's not *fair*, what I'm thinking ought to be private. I don't remember giving you permission to read my thoughts!'

He gave the very faintest of shrugs. 'I never do it intentionally, and I certainly can't do it all the time. But sometimes I look at you and just know what you're thinking. And I was right, wasn't I? You *are* going to Ashborne Hall.'

'Not that it's anything to do with you, but yes, I am,' she muttered rather resentfully at last.

'Why?'

That simple question made her flash another edgy glance at him. 'Why do you want to know?' she countered.

'Because I think it might be important,' Jay replied steadily.

It was a long time before she finally answered him. 'It's just something that I want—no, not want,' she corrected herself, 'I don't want to do it at all—but I feel that I've *got* to do it. That I'll never be able to wipe the slate completely clean and start over again if I don't.' She gave a rather impatient shrug. 'Oh, I can't explain it properly. Anyway, I shouldn't need to,' she said, scowling at him. 'You seem to know everything that's going on inside my head. You probably know the reasons even better than I do.'

'Perhaps I do,' Jay agreed. 'That's why I intend to come with you.'

At that, her eyebrows shot up skyhigh. 'Oh, no, you're not!' she retorted instantly.

'Forget about the train, we'll go in my car,' he told her, as if she hadn't even spoken. 'If the motorways are clear, we should be there by mid-afternoon.'

'Are you deaf?' Charlie demanded. 'Then I'll try shouting. *You're not coming with me*!'

'I really think you ought to keep your voice down,' Jay commented reprovingly. 'Show a little consideration for your poor suffering neighbours.'

She stared up at him in disbelief. 'It's like hitting my head against a brick wall. You just totally ignore everything I say. Anyway, what are you doing here?' she demanded. 'I thought you'd be in America by now.'

'The lecture tour doesn't begin until next week, so I'm free for the next few days.'

'Then I'd have thought you'd have spent the time working on your book,' she responded stiffly.

'The book's finished.'

'Finished?' she echoed in surprise. Then a hint of sarcasm crept into her voice. 'I suppose you found another blonde who was absolutely itching to be your temporary secretary for a couple of weeks.'

'Perhaps it's a sign of advancing years, but I don't seem able to cope with more than one blonde at a time lately,' Jay answered easily. 'Particularly when that blonde happens to be you. And, as for the book—I found an excellent lady to help me finish it. I'm sure you'd have thoroughly approved of her. She was middle-aged, incredibly efficient, and scared me half to death.'

Charlie shot him a watchful glance. 'You still haven't told me what you're doing here,' she reminded him edgily.

'No, I haven't,' he agreed amiably. 'For a start, I want to apologise for the way I over-reacted when I found out you were a journalist. Not that I approve of the way you behaved,' he added warningly. 'If there's one thing that makes me completely furious, it's people poking around in my private life without permission. When I realised how you'd lied to me, it made me even more blazingly angry. I didn't really calm down again until you were on the plane back to England. Once you were gone, though, I began to look at the whole thing in a rather different light. It occurred to me that I hadn't been strictly truthful myself—at least, not in the beginning. And, considering what you'd been through, there was probably a dozen excuses that could be made for the way you behaved.'

'None of them were really very valid,' she admitted with some shame.

'They probably seemed valid at the time,' Jay responded, with unexpected gentleness. 'But let's forget about it now. It's in the past. And it isn't the main reason why I'm here.'

'Then what is?' she asked, looking at him with fresh suspicion.

'I've had a long, hard battle with my pride and my resolution to hang on to my independence—and they both lost,' he told her wryly. 'I'm ready to admit I haven't much enjoyed the last couple of weeks. I got used to having you around twenty-four hours a day. When you suddenly weren't there any more, I found I didn't like it.'

Charlie's palms had suddenly gone damp. 'You were the one who sent me away,' she muttered, hoping he couldn't hear the sudden quaveriness of her voice.

'I know,' Jay agreed. 'But it didn't take me long to realise that was a very big mistake.'

'But you said——' She stopped abruptly. It was still painful to think of all the things he had said.

'That I didn't want a serious relationship? That I'd never met anyone who could get me hooked on the idea of a long-term commitment?' he finished for her softly. 'What I didn't know at the time was that I'd already outgrown that sort of attitude. These last few days, I've realised that's exactly what I *am* starting to want. Not with just anyone, though.'

'You mean that any old blonde won't do?' Charlie retorted, trying to ignore the dizzying pounding of her heart.

'They do say that, as a man gets older, he gets far more selective,' Jay remarked thoughtfully. 'And these last few days, I've begun to notice something rather odd. I've been walking past some spectacular blondes without even giving them a second glance.'

'That must have been a bit worrying for you,' came her slightly caustic comment.

'It certainly was. I began to wonder if I was getting jaded, if it was going to take something rather exotic to turn me on in future.'

'And what conclusion did you reach?'

'None—until I walked through your door. Then I realised that all it needed was one particular blue-eyed blonde to get my male libido back to normal again. I've wanted you ever since you first opened that door and looked at me,' he added softly.

Charlie felt her legs go incredibly weak. 'Oh—but——' She stammered to a halt, a mixture of panic and elation robbing her of any intelligible speech.

'But this isn't a good time to take this any further,' Jay said easily. 'There are more important things to be dealt with first.' He bent down and picked up her bag. 'Are you ready to leave?'

'Leave?' she repeated dazedly.

'For Ashborne Hall,' he told her firmly. 'Before we talk any more about the future, we've got to deal with the past.'

Afterwards, Charlie couldn't clearly remember any of the long drive north. Jay's car sped along the motorway at a speed which she vaguely realised was well over the legal limit, but her mind seemed to have virtually closed down. It refused to think of anything except what lay ahead of them at the end of their journey.

The call she had made to the solicitors earlier that week, telling them that she intended to spend the weekend at Ashborne Hall, meant that the house would be opened up and ready for them. She had expected to stay there alone, though, to face all the old nightmares by herself. Instead, Jay was going to be there, relaxed and confident, easily reading her mind so he would know what she was thinking—and feeling—much of the time.

So how did she feel about him being with her? Uneasy, she was forced to admit to herself at last. This was make-or-break time. Over the next couple of days, a lot of things were going to have to be resolved, one way or another. It would probably have been easier if he hadn't suddenly turned up on her doorstep like that, if he hadn't insisted on coming with her. All the same, part of her was still very glad he was here.

They hardly spoke at all during the journey. Jay seemed to know that she couldn't concentrate on any kind of conversation. Finally, they left the motorway, and she began to give him directions in a low voice as they drew nearer and nearer to Ashborne Hall.

The sky had clouded over, and a few heavy raindrops were beginning to fall. It was just like the first time she had been to the Hall, seeing it with those dark, brooding storm clouds hovering overhead, and Philip Ashborne standing in the open doorway.

Involuntarily, Charlie shivered.

'Don't worry,' Jay said at once. 'It'll be all right.'

Would it? She wondered how he could possibly be so sure. There wasn't time to ask him, though, because the car was already turning in through the impressive gateway. There was just the long drive to negotiate now, and—there it was! Ashborne Hall—the familiar grey outline, the sombre stonework, formed an impressive silhouette against the heavy, rain-laden sky.

The car crunched its way across the wide sweep of gravel in front of the house, then drew to a halt just feet away from the steps that led up to the front entrance. Jay switched off the engine, then turned and looked at her steadily.

'Come on. No use in putting it off.'

She got out slowly, hardly feeling the rain splashing on her goose-pimpled skin. Jay took hold of her arm, then firmly steered her up the steps to the massive double doors.

'How do we get in?' he asked. 'Have you got a key?'

Despite everything, Charlie gave a faint smile. 'The key to this place is so large, it looks as if it would unlock the Tower of London. Ring the bell,' she told him. 'I phoned the solicitors earlier in the week, and they've arranged for someone to be here, to let us in.'

They didn't have to wait long. A few seconds later, the door swung open and an older woman stood there, giving them a welcoming smile. 'Come on in, before you get soaked.'

Jay went straight inside, but Charlie hung back for a few more moments before reluctantly stepping into the magnificent entrance hall.

'If it's all right with you, I'll be leaving now that you're here,' the woman went on. 'I've followed Mr Grey's instructions, and the place is all ready for you. There are fresh sheets on the beds, the refrigerator's stocked with food, and the main rooms have been cleaned and aired.'

'Thank you,' Charlie said in a low voice.

The woman smiled again, fetched her coat, then let herself out through the front door. Once she had gone, the house seemed echoingly empty. Jay glanced around with a light frown.

'Very impressive, but not exactly homely,' he commented. His gaze slid knowingly over some of the paintings, then lingered on the silver and the antique furniture. 'Some of these things are worth a fortune,' he said in a neutral tone. 'If you sold them, you'd be knee-deep in money for the rest of your life.'

'I don't have any right to sell them,' she replied at once. 'They're not mine. At least, legally they are,' she corrected herself. 'But morally they belong to the Ashborne family.'

'The Ashborne family doesn't exist any more,' he reminded her.

'Then these treasures belong to the nation,' she insisted stubbornly. 'They certainly don't belong to me.'

Jay gave a brief nod, and at the same time his mouth relaxed into a faint smile. 'I'm glad I'm not marrying a fortune-hunter.'

'Marrying?' she echoed, blinking hard with a mixture of astonishment and sudden alarm.

'I think it's something we should seriously consider,' he told her comfortably. 'I seem to be getting very conventional in my old age. And marriage has a lot to recommend it. Slippers in front of the hearth, regular, well cooked meals, a good woman to warm my bed——'

'I can't cook,' Charlie muttered dazedly.

'Then I'll settle for the other two. Aren't you going to show me around?' he asked, peering interestedly into the nearest room.

It wasn't for several more minutes that it occurred to Charlie that he might be deliberately distracting her, so she wouldn't have time to brood. All the same— suggesting marriage was a rather drastic way of trying to keep her mind off less pleasant things! And had he really meant it? He *sounded* as if he had. It was so difficult to tell with Jay, though. A lot of the time, he retreated behind that bland, amiable façade, and you didn't know if he was being serious or not.

The tour of the downstairs rooms took quite some time. It was funny, but Charlie began to feel as if she was showing him around someone else's house. She seemed to be wrapped in a comforting layer of detachment; it was hard to believe that she had actually lived here for several months. Perhaps it was because Ashborne Hall had never felt like a home, but more like a very grand hotel in which she had been forced to stay for a while.

When every room on the ground floor had been inspected, Jay began to head towards the circular staircase that swept up to the first floor.

'No!' said Charlie with sudden fearfulness, abruptly swamped by an unexpected wave of pure panic.

Jay came over and linked his hand through hers. 'Don't chicken out on me now, Charlotte. You haven't come this far just to back out at the final hurdle.'

Something in his voice steadied her, and gave her back a little courage. And the firm clasp of his hand was comforting, too, making her feel as if nothing could go terribly wrong while he held her in that light grip.

All the same, her legs were shaking badly as he led her up the stairs. When they reached the first floor, her gaze slid involuntarily to the second door along, and then she couldn't look away again. Jay instantly noticed her fixed expression.

'Is that the room you shared with Philip?' he asked evenly. 'Then let's take a look inside.'

She didn't want to, but she didn't have much choice. Jay was already leading her in that direction. As he opened the door, a huge shudder vibrated through her body, but he wouldn't let her be a coward and run away. Instead, he firmly guided her inside.

It was so horribly familiar, it might have been only yesterday she had spent those last few nightmarish hours here. The massive four-poster bed with the silk covers; the antique dressing-table with its intricate gold gilding and the delicate china pots; the matching chairs with hand-embroidered cushions. Then her gaze slid back to the bed again—her marriage bed...

'Is that where it happened?' Jay asked steadily.

Charlie nodded numbly. Her throat was too dry to speak.

'Then that's where we'll sleep tonight,' he told her with quiet decisiveness.

She stared at him in total disbelief. 'Are you crazy?' she croaked, somehow finding her voice. 'I can't sleep in that bed, I *can't*! And you know why, I told you what—what Philip did! I can't even look at it without remembering, feeling sick——' And it was true; she could almost feel the point of that knife pricking her vulnerable skin, see the wild glint in Philip's eyes as he had leant over her. Her stomach was churning now in remembrance of the pure terror that had swamped her.

Jay caught hold of her shoulders, and swiftly swung her round to face him. Charlie blinked hard. For a moment, she couldn't separate his face from the memory of Philip's; they both kept swirling round and round in front of her eyes. Then slowly, very slowly, she began to focus on Jay's features. She saw his grim expression, her gaze fixed on his familiar, odd-coloured eyes, and her erratically racing heartbeat at last began to ease up just a fraction.

'Let's get a couple of things straight,' Jay said in a taut but even tone. 'I want you, Charlotte, but I want you in one piece. I don't want part of you permanently trapped in the past, haunted by old ghosts. That could easily tear our relationship apart, and I don't intend to let that happen. That's why we've got to get this settled right now and right here, where all the problems began. So—we'll get unpacked, go down and have something to eat, then come back here and go to bed. In *this* bed,' he emphasised with absolute finality. 'One way or another, I intend to finally exorcise those ghosts.'

Charlie swallowed hard. 'I'm not hungry,' she whispered. 'I couldn't eat anything.'

'I'm not sure I can, either,' Jay answered, with a dry grimace. 'Perhaps it would be better if we scrapped the preliminaries and went to bed right now.'

But she still couldn't quite believe he meant to go ahead with his insane plan, put her though such an ordeal.

'I'm—I'm not in the mood,' she muttered a little frantically.

Jay lifted one dark eyebrow. 'And you think I am? But if we can't make it work for us here, then it's never going to be completely right. So let's see what we can do about coaxing each other into the right mood, Charlotte.'

When he drew her into his arms, though, she was absolutely stiff with tension. She felt as if she was never going to be able to relax until she was out of this house, and miles away. He kissed her lightly a couple of times, but her jaw had gone quite rigid. She couldn't even open her mouth to him.

Eventually, he drew back slightly and looked down at her thoughtfully. 'There's only one way this is going to have any chance of working. You're the one who's going to have to do all the running, Charlotte. You're never going to be able to relax unless you know you're the one in charge, that you can stop if the whole thing suddenly gets more than you can cope with. That you can even run away, if you want to.'

Charlie gazed up at him through blurred eyes. 'I don't think that'll make any difference——'she began shakily.

'Try it and see,' Jay invited.

She didn't want to, but part of her knew he was right. She had come so far, battled through so much. It would be stupid to walk away now, without even making one last effort to exorcise the past, and all its horrors. Tentatively, she raised one hand and laid it flat against his chest. Then she paused for a few seconds, to gauge her reaction. Nothing too bad seemed to be happening, she finally decided. She could feel the steady beat of his heart against her palm, and somehow that seemed to be comforting. She forced herself to remember how they had touched each other when they were in South America, to recall all the pleasant sensations that had washed over her. Just for a moment, she seemed to experience an echo of that pleasure, and her body relaxed very slightly.

A little hesitantly, she slid open the buttons on his shirt. Her palm was resting against his bare skin now, crisp dark hairs brushing against her fingertips as she lightly began to stroke him. She didn't even realise her mouth had curled into the very faint shadow of a smile as she felt his heartbeat quicken and strengthen.

'Mm, nice,' Jay murmured appreciatively. 'Don't stop.'

Her hands fluttered against him a little more boldly, re-acquainting themselves with the firm, powerful outline of his body; the contrasting silkiness of his skin. And although it was the last thing she had expected, after a while she found it surprisingly easy to forget where she was; to let this big bear of a man dominate her muddled thoughts, her confused emotions, somehow sorting them all out until they made a wonderful sort of sense.

Minutes drifted past in an increasingly warm and relaxed haze. Somehow, Jay's shirt was completely off now, and there was so much more of him to slowly and slightly wonderingly explore. Almost without her realising what was happening, her hands grew bolder; touched more confidently; slid lower until she encountered fresh barriers.

'Need any help?' asked Jay with a faint grin, as her fingers hovered uncertainly over the stiff buckle of his belt.

'It might be a good idea,' she admitted a little huskily.

And after that, clothes seemed to remove themselves with incredible ease. Jay's own fingers strictly confined themselves to buttons and fastenings, though. He still hadn't touched in her return, and Charlie found her skin was beginning to tingle with frustrated anticipation.

Jay looked down at her. His face was touched with colour now, and a warm glint danced in his eyes. 'I know I told you that you had to do all the running. I don't think it's very practical, though, for you to carry me to bed.'

'Not very,' Charlie agreed in a rather dazed voice, hardly able to believe that things were going so well.

He swung her easily up into his arms, and in just two strides reached the bed. As he lowered her on to it, though, an echo of shock ran through her as she felt the familiar chill of the silk covers against her bare shoulders. For an instant, a surge of memory swept through her brain, and her body went rigid, as if bracing itself against a painful physical assault. Then she turned and saw Jay's powerful maleness sprawled out beside her, and everything gradually slid back into focus again. All the old memories simply dissolved away, as if they couldn't compete with his vibrant personality, his potent physical presence.

She propped herself up on one elbow, and stared down at him for a while, simply enjoying the sight of his strong, healthy male body. The she traced the impressive outlines of his ribcage with just the tip of one finger.

His eyes locked on to hers, and a tiny quiver ran through her as she saw the new darkness in their depths. 'Why don't you move a little closer?' he invited softly. Then he gave a small grunt of frustration as she moved just a couple of inches, tantalisingly close now but still denying him the intimate contact he craved.

'There's one thing I don't quite understand,' Charlie confessed to him in a slightly troubled voice.

Jay's right eyebrow shot up. 'You've chosen one hell of a time for a question and answer session. What do you want to know?'

'Well——' She hesitated, then blurted out, '*Why* do you want to marry me?'

His left eyebrow shot up to join the right one. 'Because I love you, of course,' he said in some surprise. 'I thought you knew that.'

'Not really,' she admitted. 'I hoped that you did, but I thought—I was worried in case you just felt sorry for me,' she went on, in a rush. 'That your conscience started to twinge after you left me, so you thought you'd better come after me, make yourself responsible for me.'

'I was definitely getting some twinges—but not from my conscience!' Jay said wryly. 'I told you—once you weren't around any more, I realised how used I'd got to you being there. That was a whole new experience for me, and it took me a while to work out the reason for it. When I finally managed it, the shock nearly hit me for six. The last thing I'd ever expected was to fall in love with you. I spent a long time trying to work out how it had happened, when it had happened. Then I thought, to hell with it! What's the point in trying to analyse something that's confounded the most brilliant brains in the world? If I loved you, then I loved you, and I'd better take it from there. It certainly shot to pieces all my neat little theories about not wanting to get involved in a long-term relationship, but it's not the first time in my life I've been totally wrong about something.' He gave a brief grin. 'Believe it or not, I'm not infallible.' Then his eyes suddenly darkened a shade and he gave a faint groan. 'Charlotte, what are you doing?'

'Moving a little closer,' she told him with some satisfaction.

One of his hands came up, and for a moment she blinked because she thought he was going to push her away from him. Instead, though, his fingers closed firmly and possessively around one of her breasts, forcing a deep shiver of delight from her as he touched her intimately for the first time. Then his other hand slid round to the small of her back. It tugged firmly, and an instant later she found herself lying on top of him, her full weight pressing against the warmth and hardness of him, her heart pounding in a crazy rhythm that matched his own.

She gazed down at him, but he didn't move; it was clear that he intended they should stay this way.

'Jay?' she questioned in a shaky whisper.

He looked up, his eyes almost black now with the sudden, fierce flare of his desire. At the same time, he slid his palms down the back of her thighs, sliding them apart and coiling them round his own. She was crushed against him, but he was the one who was a prisoner, pinned down by her weight.

'This way, you're free to run away—if you want to,' came his husky response.

The heavy beating of his blood seemed to be echoing through her own body, and the persistent throbbing was making her feverish and dizzy.

Charlie shook her head. 'I don't want to run away. And I don't want it to be like this.'

Jay studied her face searchingly. 'Sure?'

'Absolutely certain,' she somehow got out through her constricted throat.

With one easy movement, he flipped her over on to her back. Then she was aware of his powerful strength fitting itself against her, and she knew she was completely trapped, she would never be able to get away if he didn't want to let her go. But there was no trace of fear left in her now; it had been completely driven out by an overwhelming surge of love for this man. She simply closed her eyes, then revelled in the explosive sensations that were being sparked off by his need for her.

A moment later, though, Jay went very still, and she felt an unexpected wave of tension run through his huge frame.

'Look at me!' he instructed, with sudden fierceness.

Charlie forced open her heavy eyes, then fixed her blurred gaze on his strong, taut features. It wasn't until she saw the dark shadow lying across his face that she realised what the matter was. He thought she had closed her eyes because she had wanted to blot out his face! He was afraid a part of her was still trapped in the haunted horrors of her past.

'No ghosts,' she assured him in a loving whisper.

'Then say my name,' he ordered in a throaty voice, as if he didn't quite believe her.

'Jay.'

He bent his head, licked one hard tip of her breast, and then hungrily explored the outer swell with his lips.

'Say it again!'

'Jay——' she breathed, and this time there was soft pleading in her tone. He answered it by letting those powerful but gentle hands of his force exquisite sensations from her quivering body. Brand new waves of pleasure were lapping at all her nerve-ends now, everything inside her seemed wound up to an unbearable pitch, and he seemed to know it. She could feel an answering tension building up in his own raw nerve-ends, a twin echo to her own, and he was shuddering now whenever he touched her. Although he was fighting hard to control it, that great body was vibratingly close to its ultimate release.

The runaway need swept fiercely over them in a fresh and achingly compulsive surge, drawing them together like the most powerful of magnets. The last barrier was breached so easily, so naturally, that it was hard to imagine a time when they hadn't been joined in this total intimacy; then, only seconds later, without any warning, it was as if someone had hit an explosive switch that detonated simultaneously inside both of them. Charlie felt as if she was being flung to the far reaches of the universe, only drifting back slowly, oh, so slowly, finally landing back on the rumpled bed with the softest of thumps. Dazedly, she lay there with Jay's weight still sweetly crushing her, feeling as if she might never be able to move her languid body again.

Finally, she found just enough strength to move her head and gaze up at him, only to find he was looking equally stunned and disorientated.

'I think this is where I say "wow!",' she whispered shakily.

'You're lucky to have enough strength to say anything at all,' Jay responded, equally breathlessly.

Charlie curled up a little closer. 'It's hard to believe I was so scared of something so fantastic,' she murmured dreamily, feeling as if she wanted to purr like a cat with pure contentment.

'It was good, wasn't it?' he agreed, with just a touch of male smugness. 'Although I didn't mean it to be over *quite* so quickly,' he added, slightly ruefully. 'I do have my reputation to think of!'

Charlie laughed. 'I don't think your reputation's suffered at all. In fact, I'll give you a written testimonial, if you like.'

'Just keep looking at me the way you are right now,' he told her softly. 'That's testimonial enough for any man.'

They lay silently for a long while, warm and comfortable and close. Then Jay stirred slightly, raising himself on one arm so he could gaze down at her.

'Now that I've got you with your guard down, I think I'll follow up my advantage and get our plans for the future straightened out. I know you resigned from *Tomorrow* magazine, but have you made any other plans? Apart from marrying me, of course,' he added firmly, as if there were no question of her refusing him.

Charlie flushed with pleasure at his possessive tone. 'I thought I might try working free-lance for a while, see how that works out,' she told him.

'Then you'll be free to come to America with me next week?'

For a few seconds, her heart thudded joyfully at the prospect. Then her face clouded over, and she bit her bottom lip.

'I can't. I——' She hesitated, then rushed on, 'I'm going into hospital.'

Jay looked at her with a quick frown of concern. 'What for?'

'I saw a plastic surgeon,' Charlie explained. 'He—he thinks he can do something about my scars.' She met his gaze anxiously, praying he would understand.

He didn't answer straight away. Instead, he lightly ran his finger over the thin, white marks that patterned her upper chest.

'You don't have to have it done because of me,' he said steadily, at last. 'I don't give a damn about those scars.'

'I know that,' Charlie answered gratefully, and it was true. She was absolutely certain he wouldn't care if she was marked from head to foot. 'But I'd already decided to have it done before—well, before you came back. And now—I still want it done. I want to be perfect for you,' she confessed shyly.

Jay leaned forward and kissed her lightly but very thoroughly, his lips and tongue reassuring her that he would always love her, no matter what she looked like. 'You're already perfect,' he told her gently. 'But if you're determined to go through with this, I'll cancel the lecture tour so I can be there with you.'

She shook her head at once. 'No, there's no need for that. I can face it on my own. Thanks to you, there isn't anything in the world I'm scared of now. I can certainly cope with a few weeks of surgery.' She paused, then added, 'Are you still planning on going to California, after you've finished the tour?'

He nodded. 'I've already been in touch with my sister. She says I'm welcome to stay with her as long as I please. Or she'll rent an apartment for me, if that's what I prefer.'

'Then let's meet in California,' Charlie suggested. 'You'll have finished the lecture tour, and I'll be over the surgery by then. We'll both be free to get on with our lives.'

Jay gave a displeased growl. 'But that means we'll be apart for several weeks. Do you know what that's going to do to me, being away from you that long?'

'Just think how pleased you'll be to see me,' she said with an impish grin.

He grunted in frustration, but didn't argue with her any more. Instead, one powerful leg coiled round her, trapping her against him, and a second later she let out a small squeak of surprise as his tongue found a highly sensitive spot, then began to ruthlessly lick her into submission.

'Jay? Jay!' she got out breathlessly, torn between a rather pleasant sense of shock and sudden melting delight.

'No use fighting it, sweetheart,' he told her amiably. 'Since we'll be going our separate ways as soon as we leave here, I've decided to make the most of these few hours we've got together.'

And she didn't bother to argue with him, partly because she didn't want to, and partly because, in just seconds, he had reduced her to total speechlessness with his clever, loving hands and mouth.

Charlie descended the steps of the plane, and felt the warm California sunshine beating against her skin. She knew that, outwardly, she looked calm and composed. Inside, though, she was more nervous than she had ever been in her life before. Despite Jay's phone calls, letters and flowers while she had been in hospital, she still couldn't quite believe he would be here, waiting for her. This was California, wasn't it, where they had the most beautiful blondes in the world? What if he had found one he liked better than her? One who was more gorgeous, more experienced, more—oh, more everything!

Her legs carried her unsteadily towards the airport building. She could see groups of people waiting to meet the plane, but they all looked so ordinary. Her gaze flicked over them without seeing the familiar face she was looking for.

Then there was a slight disturbance at the back. A great bear of a man was impatiently pushing his way through to the front, one green eye and one blue eye intently scanning the passengers, and then lighting up brightly as they finally fixed on her.

Seconds later, she was in his arms, nearly crushed by an enormous hug.

'If you ever leave me again,' Jay threatened huskily a few minutes later, 'I might not be responsible for the consequences!'

'I won't leave you,' she promised. Then she glanced around. 'It looks as if everyone else has left. I suppose we ought to be going, too. Where are we going to stay?'

'With my sister for a few days, until we're married. Then I've taken a short lease on an apartment. I've decided that we definitely need some privacy after the wedding,' he told her meaningfully, making her first blush, then laugh with sheer pleasure.

'Are we really getting married in just a few days?' she asked, still not quite able to believe it.

'Everything's arranged,' Jay assured her, with deep satisfaction. 'I thought we'd stay in California for a while afterwards. I want a *very* long honeymoon—and I've all sorts of plans for how we'll spend the time,' he added in a voice that was heavy with promise. 'And when it's finally over—if we've enough strength to stagger out of bed,' he said, with a huge grin, 'I thought we'd fly north, to Canada, so you can introduce your new husband to your mother. How does that sound?'

'Perfect,' Charlie said happily. 'Absolutely perfect.'

And that's exactly how it was.

In the 1870s the Wild West was no place for a refined young woman from Boston

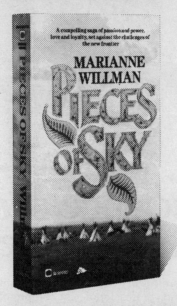

Norah O'Shea was a beautiful and refined city girl. Lured by the call of the New Frontier, she leaves the monotonous boredom of Boston and heads for Arizona and her mail-order husband – a man she has never even seen.

Seeking romance and adventure, she soon discovers all her dreams are shattered by the unforeseen hardship and heartache of this uncivilised land.

Pieces of sky • Price £2.95 • Published April 1988

W●RLDWIDE

Available from Boots, Martins, John Menzies, W. H. Smith, Woolworths and other paperback stockists.

Conscience, scandal and desire.

A dynamic story of a woman whose integrity, both personal and professional, is compromised by the intrigue that surrounds her.

Against a background of corrupt Chinese government officials, the CIA and a high powered international art scandal, Lindsay Danner becomes the perfect pawn in a deadly game. Only ex-CIA hit man Catlin can ensure she succeeds… and lives.

Together they find a love which will unite them and overcome the impossible odds they face.

Available May. Price £3.50

W⦿RLDWIDE

Available from Boots, Martins, John Menzies, W.H. Smith, Woolworths and other paperback stockists.

Mills & Boon COMPETITION

How would you like a year's supply of Mills & Boon Romances **ABSOLUTELY FREE?**

Well, you can win them! All you have to do is complete the word puzzle below and send it into us by **30th June 1988**

The first five correct entries picked out of the bag after that date will each win a year's supply of Mills & Boon Romances (Ten books every month – worth over £100!) What could be easier?

```
S L O V E S O R M I R P P
N E P U C R E T T U B A A
O E L B Y P P O P L S N
W O A K L U P I N O U S Y
D M V C C S L R W C C Y
R I E T O U H I M A O A
O T N I T W S S L L R I
P E D D A I S Y L I C L
S L E A N D B L E L E H
O O R C H I D O I N S A
L I L Y A L O I V P O D
N V L I D O F F A D R H
```

Lavender	Rose	Primrose	Cowslip
Honeysuckle	Tulip	Snowdrop	Lilac
Buttercup	Iris	Orchid	Lupin
Crocus	Daisy	Dahlia	
Poppy	Violet	Pansy	**PLEASE TURN**
Daffodil	Viola	Lily	**OVER FOR**
			DETAILS
			ON HOW
			TO ENTER

How to enter

All the words listed overleaf, below the word puzzle, are hidden in the grid. You can find them by reading the letters forwards, backwards, up or down, or diagonally. When you find a word, circle it, or put a line through it. After you have found all the words, the left-over letters will spell a secret message that you can read from left to right, from the top of the puzzle through to the bottom.

Don't forget to fill in your name and address in the space provided and pop this page in an envelope (you don't need a stamp) and post it today. Hurry – competition ends <u>30th June 1988</u>

Only one entry per household please.

Mills & Boon Competition,
FREEPOST,
P.O. Box 236,
Croydon,
Surrey CR9 9EL.

Secret message _____

_____

Name_____

Address_____

_____

_____

_____Postcode_____

COMP 4